The Joy of Drumming

Drums & Percussion Instruments from Around the World

Töm Klöwer

Binkey Kok Publications,
Diever, Holland

First published in English in 1997 by
Binkey Kok Publications
Kruisstraat 4
Diever 7981 AR
HOLLAND
Fax: 31 521 591925

Distributed to the trade in the U.S.A. by
Samuel Weiser, Inc.
Box 612
York Beach, ME 03910-0612

CIP-DATA KONINKLIJKE BIBLIOTHEEK, DEN HAAG

Klöwer, Töm
  The Joy of Drumming / Töm Klöwer
  [transl. from the German by Tony Langam and Plym Peters.;
  photos: Barbara Busch; musical notation, illustrations: Töm
  Klöwer & Michael Köttner].-Diever; Binkey Kok. - Ill.,   photos
  Transl. of: Trommels & Klankinstrumenten - Diever Holland,
  Binkey Kok, 1996.
  ISBN 90-74597-31-9
  Subject headings: Music/Drums/Creativity

Layout: RGA 2000, Bureau voor grafische productie
Cover design: Jaap Koning BNO

Typeset in 10 point Times

Printed and bound in Holland
01 00 99 98
10 9 8 7 6 5 4 3 2

Dedicated to my son David,
and all those who believe in the creative aspects of man.

Contents

Part 5 Percussion Techniques and Rhythms

Appendix

Acknowledgments

I would like to express my thanks to: Mustapha Tettey Addy and all the African teachers who enriched me with their drumming; Rolf Exler, who helped me so well to assimilate and make creative use of my intense experiences in Africa; students of drumming for being prepared and patient enough to learn with me; Dudu Tucci, Martin Verdonk, John Santos and Nicita D'Avila, who introduced me to the musical world of Afro-Brazilian and Afro-Cuban culture, and made a big contribution to this book with their inspirational and interesting discussions; Reinhard Flatischler, who showed me the totalitarian path to rhythm; Glen Velez, whose style of playing on the frame drum made a great impression on me and inspired me in a completely new way; Johannes Heimrath, for his knowledge and individual method of working with gongs in music therapy; Hans Mensing, who taught me the power of silence, and all the others who have supported me, looked after me, helped me, and stimulated me to write this book.

Silence is the cradle of all sounds

Foreword

A world without music is unimaginable. Music effects the deepest layers of the psyche and influences our life every day. For some people, it is the vehicle that takes them away from unpleasant reality; while for others it is a path to the self. Sadly, I often hear people say, "I'm not musical." This is a tragedy because music is such a fundamental form of human expression. But there are no truly unmusical people. Everyone can be creative and full of vitality. The limited use of creativity and personal vitality has been brought on by social values that overemphasize the importance of commercial tangibles while overlooking the intangible wealth of artistic expression. Many people have very little confidence in their own artistic powers because they feel imprisoned by physical and psychological limitations acquired from an education that doesn't relate to real life and the expression of emotion and spirituality. Music carries the energy of the deepest human experiences and stimulates physical and psychological vitality. Music encourages emotional expression and is the link between the inner and outer world. Our spiritual development toward a life of synergy depends on the extent to which we can restore the normal functions music had, as a matter of course, in earlier times. We will have to find ways of doing this in our time. It is my hope, with this book, to contribute to this goal by getting you involved in the most fundamental aspect of music-making: connecting to your innate sense of rhythm, and bringing it forth in shaking, rattling, rolling, joyful drumming!

Drums and sounding instruments—including gongs—have a special influence on listeners among all primitive peoples; they have always known and used drums to affect the body and the subconscious. Scientific research is now exploring and confirming the physical, mental, and emotional influence of percussion. Powerful force-fields of sounds and tones can transport us to different regions of consciousness and stimulate physical energy. That is why sound and rhythm have a nourishing, psychological, and physical appeal. I interpret the enormous interest in percussion as a search for an encounter with the inner forces of music. The growing demand for percussion and sound effect instruments is a symptom of our need to recover access to the nourishing power of music.

Drums are not solely played in Africa, and the sound of the gong is not confined to Asia; they have been incorporated in music all over the world for a long time. The enormous wealth of sounds from percussion instruments astonishes and fascinates nearly everyone. What, exactly, is the special character of a percussion instrument? Apart from its often rather exotic appearance, it is, above all, the timbre or "color" of the sound that strikes the imagination. This is percussion's great charm: its timbre carries messages from the soul.

You don't have to be a creative genius with a natural sense of pitch to take part in making music with others. In this book, you will find a survey of percussion instruments—traditional, popular, recently developed, and trend-setting instruments—from many different cultures. At least one of these delightful instruments will appeal to those of you who want to enter the world of drums and sounding instruments, and who would like to know about the sounds and creative possibilities of percussion instruments. Those of you who are already working as musicians in music therapy and/or education will find inspiring new instruments—as well as ancient instruments with which you may have been unfamiliar—to use in your work. With practical examples, this book also provides a basic knowledge of rhythm and musical inspiration for you to begin your journey through the world of drums and percussion instruments.

"Strike a membrane with a stick, the ear is filled with noise—an unmelodious, inharmonic sound. Strike it a second time, a third, you've got rhythm." [1]

[1]   Mickey Hart with Jay Stevens, *Drumming at the Edge of Magic: A Journey into the Spirit of Percussion* (SanFrancisco: HarperSanFrancisco, 1990) p. 12.

Music chases away sadness and fear by stimulating the vital forces.
—A saying of the Dogon tribe from Nigeria.

Part 1

The Magical World of Music and Percussion

The Power of the Drum

The drum, one of the oldest instruments, is a member of the membranophones, a group of instruments that produces tones through the vibration of a stretched skin or membrane. Ancient illustrations show that there were drums 4,000 years ago in Mesopotamia and Egypt. Many ethnic cultures attribute a ritual and shamanic significance to the drum. It was beaten in celebrations or to call upon the gods. Drums were also used to send signals or messages, or they accompanied singing and dancing. Since the 18th century, drums and timpani have also been included in the symphony orchestra. The drum is a powerful instrument for human expression, and was used in sacred places, as well as on historical battlefields. In his book, *Drumming at the Edge of Magic*, Mickey Hart wrote: "Drums were the driving force behind the percussive din that permeated the ancient art of warfare. The name of the game was to energize your troops while terrifying your enemies with the heroic quality of the noise you could make." [2] In addition to being an important part of communication and ancient healing and religious ceremonies, the drum is also found in secular and festive celebrations, such as sports events, Carnival, and Mardi Gras.

The drum produces a very primitive sound (the heartbeat), and has a distinctive appearance (round, like the world). It embodies both male and female principles; the body of the instrument is the female, sounding, receptive, bearing principle, while the skin is the male, giving, active, penetrating, conceptual principle. Together, the skin and the body form a whole new entity from their creative and receptive essences.

The sound and rhythm of drumming is of elementary importance to humankind. Stimulating spontaneous expression and providing playful possibilities for non-verbal communication, percussion is a valuable tool in music therapy, as well as art. In modern society, we live with a great deal of emotional and ideological restraint, as well as suppressed creativity, which puts us in danger of spiritual impoverishment or inner death. Creativity returns us to the resonating area of the soul that seeks to grow and express itself, and harmonize the energy of the body. Drumming is one of the simplest, most direct ways of accessing creative energy.

---

[2]   Mickey Hart with Jay Stevens, *Drumming at the Edge of Magic: A Journey into the Spirit of Percussion* (San Francisco: HarperSanFrancisco, 1990) p. 78.

Rhythm is very powerful, alive, dynamic, and natural. Rhythm can be heard everywhere, in the rushing of the sea or in birdsong. Rhythm is concealed in every sound, in every note and tone. In physical terms, sound is vibrating air. Vibration is movement. Anyone who has ever looked at the sea can see one wave following another. The repetition of this process within a particular time creates a rhythm. In between, there are rests and moments of silence. If this process were to take place faster, so that the movement was condensed, the rhythm of the waves would change into a sound or a note. The ear would no longer perceive the rapid rhythm of separate vibrations, but would recognize it as a particular sound. The rhythm is concealed in this sound. Rhythm is present in every aspect of life and work.

A Personal Experience

My own journey into the world of drums and percussion instruments started with a dream I had in 1984. I dreamed about Africa, an immense landscape, with large palm trees waving on the horizon and thunder in the air. At that time I was playing the saxophone in several bands, earning my living by giving lessons, as well as working another job on the side. I was fascinated by the world of jazz and blues. I had read several books about it, and was impressed by the rhythmic power of this African-American music. My interest in the musical culture of Africa had been awakened. I wanted to know how the Africans lived, how they thought, how they expressed rhythm. I wanted to discover the roots of the blues, rock-n-roll, and jazz. At the same time, I was shocked to discover that this music was the result of colonial oppression, which still exists in some parts of the world today. Early jazz can be seen as the African-American people's attempt to retain consciousness of their own roots and to escape from white doctrine and control. Now I know that Africa has helped me to rediscover my own roots and rhythms.

When I landed in Ghana in the winter of 1984, I found exactly the landscape that I had seen in my dream. I knew I had arrived at the right place at the right time. I had left everything behind me, I had abandoned my familiar world. Here, everything was unknown, different, and dark. I had started on an adventure with myself—an adventure born from the desire to experience myself differently—to break through the shackles of everyday life and the rigid routines and forms of expression.

The intense odors, the sultry climate, the many sounds of the night, the hospitality of the Ghanaians, their body language—all these things filled me with admiration and childlike amazement. The drive through Accra was like a trip through a witch's cauldron. Everywhere there were black people by the side of the road, selling all sorts of things. There was a great deal of hubbub and a lot of laughing. The people expressed their thoughts and feelings with their bodies; they liked to touch each other. Their way of walking and looking aroused my curiosity. I saw many children and adults sweeping the street with bundles of dried grasses. They usually worked on their haunches, or sitting down. Women with large platters full of fruit or breads balanced on their heads walked slowly past me. It was impressive to see how they balanced the enormous dishes, while they did other things with their hands. Then I went to a stall and ate my first deep-fried sweet potato.

When I was sitting with my drum on the first day, learning my first rhythm, after a while I felt physical strength and pleasure. It was rather like waking up or being reborn. Although I was a stranger in this country, I still felt it was my home for the time being, an emotional home, because what I experienced at that time was my own creative, playful aspect. At 8 o'clock in the morning, I had my first contact with African dance, accompanied by two drums. Drums and singing are one in the music of Africa. Dance stimulates the sense of community and feeling of solidarity. The intense and long period of dancing was an important experience for me. It was the most profound encounter I had ever had with my body.

In the evening, Mustapha Tettey Addy often gave small concerts on his family's farm. Suddenly, many of the people who had been working on the land during the day would be standing behind a drum or playing a bell. Music is at the focus of social life. The people sing, dance, drum, and laugh a great deal. According to an African proverb, "A village without music is a dead place." It seems to me that this sentiment is worth reflecting upon.

Order in Chaos

In addition to my visit to the drum school in Ghana, I was able to participate as an observer in a number of ceremonies and festivities. I was most impressed by the perfect interaction of the drummers and dancers, driven by their powerful songs. Not a drumbeat or movement is arbitrary; they are all part of a conscious choreography. To an inexperienced observer, this scenario makes a rather chaotic impression, which might lead to some incorrect interpretations, and, sometimes, to a rejection and dismissal of African cultural values. What might look like musical chaos during a drumming ritual is, in fact, a clever alternation of rhythms in polyrhythmic patterns. The deliberate way in which it progresses in detail results in a sacred dancing opera, which can only be fully understood by a participant. In his book *Muntu*, Janheinz Jahn quotes Alfons Dauer, to whom we owe the following insight: "The difference between our rhythmic conception and that of the Africans consists of the fact that we perceive rhythm by hearing, while they perceive it by movement. In this off-beat technique of the African we have before us an ecstasy in the truest sense of the word; for its essence is to disturb the static self-contained repose which distinguishes both metre and rhythm in addition to their character as time-spans. This it does by overlaying their static accents with ecstatic emphases, producing tensions between the two. The same thing happens in all forms of African combinations of rhythm; it should probably be considered their true aim and meaning. From this point of view the innermost object of African music consists in producing, through rhythmic configurations of a specific kind, an uninterrupted ecstasy."[3] The movements of the dance are not arbitrary, but are directly linked to the rhythmic patterns created by the drummers.

In order to make rhythm tangible at a musical level, humans invented meter and beat. These create order by providing a way to understand rhythm and a common language so musicians can communicate with each other. In each culture, rhythm is expressed a unique way, as a manifestation of the culture's collective philosophy. The African funeral dirge—in which the imploring sound of a drum rhythm ensures that the pain of departure is externalized and released—and the European funeral march—with its rigid

---

[3]   Janheinz Jahn, Muntu: *African Culture and the Western World* (New York: Grove Weidenfeld, 1961) p. 38.

meter, holding on to the pain of loss—reflect two distinctly different cultural attitudes toward death.

It is also interesting to compare the expression of certain European rhythmic patterns with that of Latin American rhythms. The most basic forms of rhythms are the two and three-beat bar, which developed from the two stages of the heartbeat and the three stages of breathing. The musical expression of these is known in European music as the march (two-beat) and the waltz (three-beat), as opposed to the samba (two-beat) from Brazil and the 6/8 rhythm (three-beat) from Cuba. One of the striking differences between the rhythmic styles is the placement of emphasis. In a march, the first beat of the bar is emphasized. The rhythmic basis of the samba is created by emphasizing the second beat, which is also referred to as the large "off-beat" (see Part 4). The off-beat emphasis gives the rhythm a lively character. In a march, the rhythm has a heavier, plodding sound.

Well-known musical idioms—blues, jazz, rock, soul, reggae, salsa, samba, tango, pop, etc.—have developed from many different musical worlds, with roots in different countries. The message contained in these musical forms, apart from diversity and interconnection, is that it is worthwhile to look beyond our own spiritual and cultural boundaries. On the other hand, we should remember that many of these musical forms were developed by the underprivileged, to survive and fight against an atmosphere of social repression. Music can remove social distinctions, as the history of rock music has demonstrated. Today, the African heritage is present in most of these combinations of musical styles, and its most important contribution to these styles is the great diversity of rhythms and musical complexity.

Polytheism

The polyrhthmic nature of African music echoes African religious belief in many different gods. In colonial times, European missionaries' imposition of their monotheistic view of the world contributed to the suppression of African culture, but at the same time it instigated the rise of various syncretic religions, following the subjugation of the indigenous black populations. The attempts of missionaries to replace the African gods with a single god succeeded only superficially. The slaves assimilated elements of the Catholic religion, integrating the Catholic saints and holy days into their shamanic religion, so they could continue to honor the traditional African spiritual forces. This long process of the fusion of religions resulted in the syncretic religions of Cuban Santeria and Brazilian Candomble, to name a couple. Both contain a mixture of ancient Yoruba rites and elements of Catholicism. Thus, as their traditions and customs demanded, Africans in the New World were able to serve the ancient and "new" gods. African polytheism is prepared and open to including different gods in its pantheon, and to perform the related ceremonies. The essence of the African way of life is the communal aspect, the link between the individual and the community—the acceptance of duality within the whole.

In African music, it is quite natural to find, for example, a three-beat rhythm being played over a two-beat rhythm. Each rhythmic pattern has its own emotive power; three-beat rhythms have a light, happy sound, while two-beat rhythms have a somber sound. Both joy and sadness can be present at the same time, and the one does not have to exclude the other. Western culture tends to look at joy and sadness as mutually exclusive feelings. However, contrasts are constantly present and influence our lives every second. If we can embrace this polarity, we live in unity. African philosophy and music have inspired me to think about this, to reflect on my own duality and how it prevents unity and divides my thoughts into concepts such as "good" and "bad."

What we believe is not as important as believing in something, without being fanatical. Believing means approving, trusting in something that gives us strength. When we communicate or make contact with something that is superhuman—divine—we connect with primeval forces. If we see religion (Latin: *religare*, to tie fast) in such a way that it does not bind or restrict our personal, subjective experiences, we are able to grow spiritually and become more consciously aware. What we believe profoundly affects our culture. For example, while the African slaves were prevented from openly worshipping their pantheon of gods, the nature of the music they created became less polyrhythmic; but after their emancipation, and as they regained the strength of their identity, polyrhythms resurfaced, most notably in jazz. Rhythms have their own dynamics and reflect aspects of human existence.

The Appeal of Ethnic Music

I think that the appeal of ethnic music is based on the laws of vibration working throughout the universe of creation. The player, as well as the dancer and the listener, become part of a physical, tangible experience, which can sometimes create a trance state that imparts a sense of connection with the world as a whole. This state of consciousness transports a person to a connection with the heartbeat of life. The feeling of being transported can be relaxing, which allows for the greatest possible resonance with a "universal power." Throughout history, man has produced rhythm and sounds that serve as a source of energy in rituals. These rituals bring about purification and healing in people, and are based on their surrender to sound. There are few ritual activities that take place without music.

For centuries, hidden behind the Sahara, African rituals and ideas were invisible counterparts to Western music. Thanks to the spirit of New Music, there is a growing awareness of non-European music—from the Far East or Africa—and the foundation has been lain for making and experiencing music in a new way. The rediscovery of the ethnic sources of acoustic instruments broke through the boundaries of classically-trained musical views and resulted in a new stage in musical consciousness, as well as a different way of thinking on spiritual and ethical levels. Suddenly it was possible to listen to the inner sound in music, to incorporate it in meditation, or to express and liberate oneself through the spectrum of sound of rhythmic, ecstatic drumming, and reach a new state of consciousness. Access to non-European music was not only a musical experience, but also resulted in the transmission of philosophies and cultural values of a completely new dimension.

In my opinion, Claude Debussy, who championed the emancipation of percussion and other sound effect instruments in European music, is among the most important catalysts for the rediscovery of the percussion instrument at the beginning of the 20th century. His first encounter with percussive music was during the World Exhibition in Paris in 1898, when he heard a Balinese gamelan orchestra and saw Indian plays; this influenced many of his compositions. Two other great composers of the time were Bela Bartok and Carl Orff. They were also precursors of music based on rhythmic percussion, and they made a valuable contribution to music education; Bartok with his piano pieces for children, and Orff with his musical model for self-discovery, in which rhythmic-melodic instruments, like the xylophone, play a central role. Many sound artists whose works prominently feature percussion instruments and alternative music styles include avant-garde composers such as Mauricio Kagel, John Cage, Karlheinz Stockhausen (electronic music), Steve Reich and Terry Riley (representatives of "minimalist music").

What attracted Westerners to explore traditional, non-European music? I believe it was this music's clearly unique timbre and its effect upon consciousness. Timbre is produced by the interplay of harmonics. Every sound and every tone consists of a number of harmonics. Some examples of dynamic harmonic interplay can be heard in the chanting of Tibetan monks, the harmonic singing from Siberia and Mongolia, the sound of the didgeridoo, the drum music of the group, Kodo, or in gamelan music.

In his book, *Through Music to the Self*, Peter Michael Hamel wrote: "Anyone who has become aware of the tone-colour or spectrum of a single tone, or who has even detected isolated overtones within a note, will keep trying to rediscover this natural phenomenon when listening to music. And in the process it will quickly become clear to him that some forms of music positively set out to make the tone-colours audible, while others encourage no such acoustic procedure." [4]

All the mystical music for one voice from India, all the heterophonic music from Indonesia, the music from the Arabic countries and the Middle Ages, as well as the drum music of Africa, is music with timbre, in so far as they allow for harmonics to be heard. In the work of Bartok, for example, the emphasis on timbre is aimed at producing vibration in the inner being, the soul. In India, even now, it is said that correct inner listening is a precondition for the player's inspiration.

Peter Michael Hamel wrote that in Europe, the influence of composers such as Karlheinz Stockhausen brought the phenomena of timbre and harmonics to the forefront of modern composers' consciousness, and has contributed to a deeper insight into the spiritually transformative power of sound. [5] The rediscovery of percussion, with its suggestive and magical sounds, took place at the same time as the introduction of new sounds (created electronically or with unconventional instruments) in Western concert halls. Audiences and professional musicians alike are attracted to experiencing new vibrations and are enthusiastic about the creative use of sounds and

---

[4]   Peter Michael Hamel, *Through Music to the Self: How to Appreciate and Experience Music Anew* (Boulder: Shambala, 1979) p. 127.

[5]   *Ibid*, p. 25

rhythms. Experiencing sound and percussion in a group, learning how percussion instruments should be used, learning about the original rhythms, dances and songs, drumming together—all of these positive experiences explain the growing interest in percussion as a musical genre.

The Percussionist

Of course, there is another very important factor which has influenced the growth in popularity of percussion music: the musicians and bands of the pop, rock, and jazz scene, such as Carlos Santana, Frank Zappa, Don Ellis, Miles Davis, Al Jarreau, Traffic, Osibisa, Sting, Prince, and many others. It was because of them that the percussive element came into its own in these musical styles.

At the same time, a new type of musician was developing: the percussionist. In the 1940s, Cuban musicians integrated the conga technique into jazzy grooves. In the 1970s, Airto Moreira fascinated Western musical culture with the enormous range of Afro-Brazilian percussion instruments. The modern percussionist is, in fact, multicultural, with access to the cultures of other countries and many resources for studying their rhythms and sounds. The percussionist plays not only the drums, such as congas or bongos, but also makes use of a large number of different instruments, such as barchimes, wood blocks, caxixis, bells, tambourines, shékere, and numerous other sound effects instruments.

One of the percussionist's tasks is to create different sounds that provide the music with a magical, atmospheric dimension. Many recordings that include a percussionist are characterized by the great diversity of the instruments' sounds. It is particularly within simple compositions of harmonic-melodic structures that percussion can realize its full range of sounds and power.

There are many interesting percussionists and drummers with different socio-cultural backgrounds and sophisticated styles of playing. They have played in well-known groups, or have developed their own projects. Their drum music can be admired on many different recordings. The discography in the appendix contains many of their names, but of course, there are many more. With their musical talent, they have popularized and enriched percussion music.

Hearing and Listening

The ear listens 24 hours a day, and is an important organ for spatial orientation. It helps us to find our way in life. With the enormous range of our sense of hearing, we can distinguish approximately 1,500 different pitches and a huge spectrum of sounds. In the early history of humanity, hearing and listening had much more importance than they have now. For ancient peoples, hearing was important for survival, because noise always meant danger, and a rustling in the bushes could mean a fight. The present predominance of sight in Westerners has developed only in the last 300 or so years, and has resulted in a one-sided orientation of consciousness. The special characteristics of hearing have clearly been neglected, and to a large extent we try to understand and analyze the world through sight. The world we see becomes an image of reality in the brain, a reconstructed misunderstanding, because what we see is not what is really there. We see only the surface of things.

The mystics of India, Tibet, Japan, and Europe have long pointed out that we do not see the world correctly. Now science is confirming this fact. It is not possible to conceive of the whole of reality. Westerners, dependent on sight, can have different experiences through the sense of hearing, and can evaluate and experience perception of the world in new ways. This changed perception influences social life. In this respect, Joachim E. Berendt describes the research of a team of American psychologists in his book, *The Third Ear*. This team compared a "radio city" in the Rocky Mountains, where atmospheric conditions make it impossible to receive transmitted television images, with a "television city," where people watched an average of six hours of television a day. In the radio city, there was clearly less criminality and fewer problems in families and schools.[6]

The ability to listen strengthens personal identity. Research has shown that people who become deaf are more likely to have psychological problems than people who go blind. The quality of listening develops from conscious awareness in hearing. Listening with awareness enhances the capacity of the ear to hear and makes a person as a whole more vital and energetic; hearing, as such, provides nourishment. The emancipation of the ear as a sensory organ contributes to a new form of thinking. The ear has the primary task of bringing energy to the brain, and this leads to a strengthening of

---

[6]   Joachim-Ernst Berendt, *The Third Ear* (New York: Henry Holt & Co., 1992) p. 167.

consciousness and a more accurate perception in comparison with that of the eye. For example, the ear can recognize the different tones of human voices at a great distance, while the eye sees shades of color merely as a black dot.

Music appeals to the capacity to hear and listen, and allows direct access to extremely personal areas that are normally concealed and controlled by the intellect and reason. Music is at the same time a means of enlarging consciousness and changing structures of perception that have become rigid. What is the deeper significance of hearing and listening to music and sounds? Through the sense of hearing, a person comes into contact with the essence of his or her existence. This essence is concealed, existing at the level of the soul. With the inner strength of pure music, this essence can be stimulated to express and articulate itself. At that point, the listener is able— with the voice or an instrument—to choose his or her own expression of those aspects which reflect personal feelings. Sounds created in this way— produced by a drum, gong or in any other way—carry messages from the sounding board of the personality to the outside world. Communication is achieved by means of the echo we produce in response. True communication means: I am listening.

Silence

What would it be like if everything were suddenly silent, if machines fell silent and the familiar noise was replaced by an acoustic void? We would find ourselves again, and perhaps we would be shocked by the inner noise of our thoughts. The fear of a quiet pause, of silence, is the fear of doing nothing, of simple existence, of the experience that what I am is sufficient. When we stop talking, we increase the possibility of silence. Silence is dependent on our being prepared to stop talking. When the noise of our thoughts disappears, when there is no longer any desire, any sense of having to do something, any will, we are left in silence.

Silence is one of the greatest teachers and invites us to listen. Anyone who can hear can attest to the feeling his or her ears move suddenly (much in the way animals' ears perk up) when a slight sound interrupts a period of silence. When I listen to the sound of rain, "I'm all ears." You could also say, "I'm all there." This is the quality of active hearing. I have become a listener. The sounds that surround me, that enter me through the inner ear, providing my cerebral cortex with energy through biochemical processes, can nourish my spirit and soul. The Hindu ragas—composed of tones, each of which are attributed to a color—are a good example of nourishing music. In addition, a specific raga is considered appropriate for a specific time of day or night, according to the energy that it generates. It's a challenge for the Westerner who is accustomed to recognizing only twelve tones, but if you listen to Hindu music, and other music based on psycho-acoustic sounds or on color, you might begin to understand what I mean by "acoustic nourishment," and it might help you move from an emphasized dependence on sight to a more refined sense of hearing.

There is silence in surrendering to the sense of hearing. John Cage, one of the leading avant-garde composers of the 20th century, studied Japanese Zen Buddhism, and discovered the power of silence through this experience. He came to believe that music sounds completely different when there is silence. In his compositions, he not only wants silence to be heard, but also uses it to give sound a new right of existence in music.

Sound and Noise

For many people, drum music is no more than noise. There is nothing that breaks through the familiar pattern of sound so completely as the sound of drums, rattles, or gongs. Mickey Hart described this phenomenon in his book, *Drumming at the Edge of Magic*. "As a drummer, I make my living producing a certain kind of vibration, a certain kind of sound. Although there are percussion instruments which can be tuned to specific pitches, most drums produce a sound that shotguns out in a wide range of pitches. This causes the drumbeat's energy to decay much faster than do sounds that are vibrating close to a single frequency, leaving us with the kind of short, sharp sound bite that is perfect for laying down a rhythm." [7]

Because of this impression of the drum's sound, drummers and percussionists are often seen as noisy people, although they are actually expressing their vitality. This noise, the creative combination of tones, sounds and rhythms, is a way of "wrapping up" silence.

What about the omnipresent noise in the street, or the noise of machines in industry, to which people are exposed every day? Or the dull thump of many types of disco music in which many people try to lose themselves, not to mention the music assailing our ears at work and in department stores? The loudspeaker is a permanent fixture in Western society, and its ubiquitous, overwhelming noise level is accepted almost without criticism. In fact, the lack of such background sounds often results in a sense of disorientation. People who are accustomed to living in noisy areas often find it difficult to sleep when they have to visit and stay or move to a quiet, peaceful area. Now we have "white noise" machines that mask over ambient, random sounds and effectively numb the mind. Since we cannot shut our ears in the way that we can shut our eyes, we must shut off inwardly. What is lost in this process is not the sense of hearing, but the inborn ability to listen. As a result, we risk becoming insensitive to the extremely important information contained in rhythms and sounds, as well as risking our physical and mental well-being.

---

[7]   Mickey Hart, *Drumming at the Edge of Magic* (San Francisco: HarperSanFrancisco, 1990) p. 27.

Music as a Cure

Music has physical effects, particularly on the pulse, breathing, muscle tension, blood pressure, and digestion. Clinical research has shown that under the influence of special music, a person's regenerative, curative processes can clearly be improved, and the amount of anesthesia needed in surgical procedures can be reduced. Stress reduction and relaxation produced by certain sounds can now be measured by an EEC (electroencephalogram). According to Chinese medicine, many physical ailments are due to either an excess or depletion of *chi* (or life energy) in certain parts of the body; music can be used to either stimulate or calm the flow of *chi*. Drumming is an especially effective way to either stimulate or calm the body's forces, and part of its effect has to do with the nature of biofeedback and the power of the mind over the body. As you drum a soft, steady rhythm, focusing on its progress, your body's rhythms move into pace with the drumming. On the same token, you can charge yourself up, or "empty" yourself out with vigorous drumming. The drum's low frequencies stimulate the motor neuron system, while its general acoustic stimuli affect the body through its sense of balance. Therefore, drums with a low frequency have a direct influence on the whole body, which vibrates, as though it is being massaged.

The universal foundation of music is rhythmic vibration. Since the beginning of life on Earth, all of us have had, as our first experience of the world, the vibrations in our mother's body, her voice, and, most importantly, her heartbeat. We learned, on an elemental level, to connect different sounds conveyed through the watery world of the womb with either safety or danger, and these experiences became imprinted in our psyches. For this reason, the fundamental structure of music is deeply connected to archetypal structures in the psyche; music can penetrate the deepest layers of consciousness. Sound and rhythm can reactivate previous physical experiences and suppressed feelings, and that is why many forms of music are used today by music therapists and doctors. Fascinating theories about the stimulation of brain waves by tones (frequencies) are giving rise to new ways of thinking about the ear as a gateway to the world of human feelings, indeed, "a gateway to the soul."

Alfred A. Tomatis is one of the most interesting pioneers of sound therapy. Tomatis' research into intrauterine life was inspired by the difficulties with his own growth in—and premature expulsion from—his mother's womb. His research affirmed that hearing is the first sense to develop, the sense through which we experience the world for the first time. He traced the foundation of how we process all experiences to our fetal experience of our mother's voice, the sounds filtered through her body, and the sounds of her body. Through this research, he created the Tomatis Method, in which the patient is guided through an acoustic rebirth. With his special auditory training program, it is possible to help people overcome psychological problems. [8]

Music is an especially effective way to process emotions, either passively or actively. A melody can bring us to tears of joy or sorrow, to the extent that it reflects our emotional state. The drum offers a projection surface for dealing with tensions and repressed emotions, centering attention, expressing aggression, and promoting self-confidence.

On an interpersonal level, music and drumming in particular provide a nonverbal way to connect with other people, a way to participate in a group energy. This naturally extends to the transpersonal level, inasmuch as the vibrations of drumming are part of the eternal rhythm of the human experience and the universe. In the world's oldest cultures, music is inextricably linked with spirituality, as an expression of humanity's highest aspirations and a vehicle for merging with the divine. It is this connection with and faith in a force that is larger and wiser than ourselves that modern Western society is so desperately in need of.

Rhythms and sounds appeal to the prelinguistic, subconscious world within a human being; this is the basis of their magic and their psychological importance. During the past decade, the ancient knowledge of how music penetrates into the deep levels of our consciousness and can revive experiences that are inaccessible to words has become increasingly significant. Monochrome sounds and monotonous rhythms can reveal biographical themes and shed light on the nonverbal qualities within in us. There is certainly a good reason why drums, gongs, rattles and other musical instruments have had a thousand-year-old religious and healing function in the cultures of all native peoples. The sound potential of these instruments has a special effect on the listener. The word "sound" is interesting in this context. It means "tone" on the one hand, but also describes health. We say we are "in sound health" when we feel strong. The relationship between sound

---

[8]   For an engaging exploration of the life and work of Alfred Tomatis, see his autobiography, *The Conscious Ear: My Life of Transformation Through Listening* (Barrytown, NY: Station Hill, 1992)

(music) and health (in the sense of being intact) is a central theme in the healing ceremonies of native people's shamanic world view.

The use of music for the holistic healing of individuals and communities is an age-old practice, as evidenced in ancient rock paintings. "We have idiophones dating back to 20,000 BC that are daubed with red ochre, a decoration most scholars believe indicates a sacred usage. But the first "document" of percussion's connection with the sacred doesn't show up until the Middle Paleolithic, around 15,000 BC, when an anonymous artist, working in a limestone cavern in Southwestern France, painted our first known picture of a musician. Known as the dancing sorcerer (or shaman) of Les Trois Frères—a cave named for the three brothers who discovered it—this picture has been interpreted by scholars as representing a man wearing the skin of an animal and playing some kind of instrument, possibly a sounding bow or concussion stick.'[9] The Old Testament of the Bible describes a music-therapy session in which David healed Saul of "an evil spirit from God" by playing on the lyre. [10]

Looking at the drum's importance in art and music therapy, it's clear that the drum has been used since time immemorial as a regular part of healing traditions, where it was used in religious ceremonies, accompanied by singing and dancing. Small clay statuettes, playing round frame drums have been found in the ruins of Ur, dating back to 2000 BC. There are various types of shamanic drums, yet the most commonly used are frame drums (see page 42). These instruments, called *duff, tar* or *doira* in the southern and eastern Mediterranean region, were brought to Europe and became known there as the tambourine, which is a popular instrument even today. In Ghana, people play on frame drums that are square and often very large; and round frame drums with wooden or clay handles are a familiar sight in many parts of Africa.

The frame drum is inseparably connected with the shamanic practices and rituals in all of Central Asia, from Tibet to Northern Siberia, as well as those of the Eskimos and Native Americans, who originally came from Northeastern Siberia. In Mongolia, for example, where the horse figures prominently in this culture's nomadic collective consciousness, the shaman plays and "rides" his frame drum (which then becomes a type of holy heavenly horse) on his "flights" after other, supernatural beings. The frame drum

---

[9] Mickey Hart, with Jay Stevens. *Drumming on the Edge of Magic: A Journey to the Heart of Percussion* (San Francisco: HarperSanFrancisco, 1990) p. 70.

[10] I. Samuel 16:15 – 16:23.

is indispensable, both as a ritual object and as an instrument that is beaten during the ceremony, for successfully carrying out the ritual.

These religious ceremonies were aimed at strengthening physical and spiritual powers, and, ultimately, aimed at the reconciliation of demonic forces and the subconscious. The shaman, or priest, was the medium between the cosmic world and humans. Serving as a drummer, healer, and master of trance, the shaman understood the essence of the drum, and its ability to evoke a strong emotional participation among the participants in the ceremony. The shaman used the drum, on the one hand, to call up the spirits or the gods, so that they could take control of a dancer's body (as in voodoo ceremonies), or put the dancer in a trance, while on the other hand, the shaman used the drum as a vehicle to submerge himself in the spirits' world via ecstatic trance. With this trance technique, the shaman is able to penetrate different levels of consciousness, to communicate with the world of spirits, and retrieve important messages for the community.

The word "trance" comes from the Latin verb "transire," and means "to go through something." I believe that anyone can experience the trance state and can have access to sources, inner regions, and healing forces that are not present in everyday consciousness. Trance states can help one experience one's self and make contact with one's own essence.

In Africa, a great variety of drums are employed in rituals. In addition to the frame drums, there are also barrel drums with one or two membranes and greatly differing forms that are used. Shamanic music differs from African music in its conception of rhythm. The shamanic rhythm is basically monotonous and does without off-beats or polyrhythmic forms. By comparison, African music emphasizes an off-beat and superimposed rhythmic structures, which is more conducive to larger groups of people joining together in various dance patterns. However, the meaning and purpose remain the same despite the different metric and rhythmic interpretation: developing a trance situation within a ritual that initiates a change of perception, thereby creating an expansion of consciousness.

There are shamanic techniques that are now being employed to access inner regions of the psyche, as well as to tap into our innate creativity. One form of shamanic drumming that has become familiar is theta drumming, which developed the U. S. A. An even, monotonous drumming of about 4-1/2 beats per second can create theta brain waves. Theta waves, the rate of which vibrate between 4 to 8 hertz, occur naturally in the realm between waking consciousness and sleep. Today, the shaman's tasks can be recognized in those of the musician and therapist, who can induce these states of consciousness and help us interpret and put into use the knowledge we bring back from them. Music has the task of opening the human being to experiences beyond the everyday situations and worldly bonds. It leads into direct experiencing, past the boundaries of logic.

The very nature of Western life, which demands that we get up and go during times when our own biological clocks tell us we should be resting, sets us apart from our natural rhythms. Many people suffer silently as a result of the restrained expression of their feelings and thoughts, as well as the suppression of their creativity. Western education focuses primarily on developing individuals who will be economically viable participants in a society that doesn't view musical knowledge as a requirement. Colleges require us to take at least a year of a foreign language, but very few require us to learn a musical instrument. A child's natural tendency to beat on things and sing little songs frequently falls into his or her family's memory of cute things that the child did. Most Westerners find the thought of expressing themselves on an instrument without having learned to play it to be unimaginable, so music tends to be associated more with performance than with fun and playing, and as "non-musicians," we tend to experience performance anxiety when "confronted" with a musical instrument. The loss of inner freedom of movement and the sense of trust in the experience of one's own rhythmic patterns causes inner despair and the accumulation of stress. In addition, because of the pressure to be a material success, or to keep a job, we often suffer from isolation or separation from creative processes. Life energy becomes frozen when we do not have an opportunity to express ourselves, to be artistically creative, and to dance. How can we change this? By bringing the ancient power of music back into our lives, beginning with the fundamentals of rhythm. Drumming is a powerful antidote for stagnant energy. It's time for each of us to pick up a magical instrument and do our part to free up the vital energy in the world!

Part 2

The Drums

A Pantheon of Drums

On the following pages, I describe 41 small and large types of drum, from Africa, Brazil, America, Asia, and the Middle East, as well as their different constructions and playing techniques. I have included both original instruments as well as modern adaptations. The drums come in all sorts of shapes (cylindrical, conical, hour-glass, or beaker-shaped), and are made of wood, metal, or fiberglass. Drums can be played with the hands, or beaten with a variety of beaters and sticks. With a few exceptions, all the instruments can be easily obtained (see the resource list in the Appendix), and are therefore available for all types of music.

There are many instruments for you to choose from here, but in my opinion, the conga is the most suitable instrument for beginners in the world of rhythm and percussion. Part 5, Rhythms, describes the conga playing technique in detail; this technique can also be used for other drums in this book.

When you are actually learning a drum rhythm, there are two demands on you at the same time. Apart from the process involved in learning the rhythm, you also have to devote attention to the technical aspects of playing, and this can sometimes be too much if you're a beginner. Therefore, before you actually start playing the drums, begin by reading Part 4, Rhythm Basics. It includes several exercises that you can do without an instrument, to get you started. They will give you a basic understanding of rhythm, so that you will better understand the various rhythms presented in Part 5, as well as learn to play other instruments more quickly.

When you start playing an instrument, it's a good idea to ask yourself what you want and expect from it. If you haven't used a percussion instrument before, adopt the approach of just allowing things to happen to you. See what your hands want to do and how your body wants to move. Feel confident about what you are doing and experiencing. When you strike a drum or sounding instrument, it's a very immediate experience. I invite you to share this experience.

Hand Drums

Djembé

This drum's origins are in Guinea, although its shape originates from the East. Djembé music is played primarily in Guinea, Senegal, and the Ivory Coast. Djembés are made in different sizes. Each drum is constructed from a single piece of a West African hardwood called "win," and it is surrounded by a simple tensioning system attached to a goatskin drumhead, so it can be tuned. The combination of African construction with Western materials, such as pre-stretched string and welded iron rings, is quite new. In addition to djembés made of wood, there are fiberglass models. Fiberglass panels, covered with layer upon layer of polyester resin, are stuck to a basic frame, which is joined with resin to another covered frame to make a single case. A floating tensioning system is used on djembés made of synthetic materials. The counter hoop is not screwed down, but welded to an iron ring, which is sunk into the bowl of the drum.

Traditionally, the bass stroke plays an important technical role in djembé music; it is created by the calyx-like shape of the sound box which allows for a higher degree of compression, giving the djembé a large, dynamic range of frequencies. In contrast with the conga, the way in which this drum is played is more open. The sounds produced by single drumbeats are rich in crystal-clear harmonics.

Adama Dramé, the master of the djembé, knows how to make it talk. In the tradition of West African drum music there are certain rhythmic patterns that correspond to letters. By joining these patterns together, it is possible to produce sentences. In this way, a solo drummer can call a dancer by drumming her name and inviting her to dance.

Kpanlogo and Oprente Drum

These two drums come from Ghana in West Africa and were used for traditional rhythms such as the Kpanlogo, Djigbo, Kpacha, Fume-Fume, Tigari, Gahu or Agbadja. The handmade wooden sound boxes of the drums are carved from a tree trunk, and the surfaces are decorated with attractive, carved designs. The oprente is a typical beaker drum, while the kpanlogo is a single-sided barrel drum.

The hide used for these drums is antelope skin. The traditional African system is used to stretch the skin with string attached to a number of wooden pegs, in contrast with the Western system made of hardware. A metal ring around the skin is attached with strings, which are pulled down by the pegs, so that the antelope skin is stretched taut. These typical Ghanaian drums are characterized by a warm, round sound, produced by the soft skin. In contrast with the conga, the African drums are shorter.

Darbukka

This hand drum is Arabian in origin, and is played in Turkey, the Balkan countries, and North Africa. Its shape and size are reminiscent of the African djembé, and yet the sound and way in which it is played are quite different. The darbukka (or darabuka), which is placed on the left leg in the Arab posture, is about 18 inches tall and has a diameter of about 10 inches. The modern version of the drum has a body made of aluminum, and is sometimes covered in brown synthetic leather. The tensioning ring is also made of aluminum, and fits snugly around the body of the drum, giving the impression that the drum is made from a single piece. The synthetic drum head is held in place by six allen screws, because it requires a great deal of tension to achieve the characteristic sound of the darbukka and get the best results from the full range of subtle playing techniques. The wealth of sounds produced by using different finger techniques gives the darbukka its magic. Some of the well-known basic strokes are the banging strokes on the edge, the bass strokes in the middle of the drum, and the sharp slaps. This drum is representative of a culture in which irregular rhythms are common.

Batá

Batá drums, which have a drumhead on both ends, are played by the Yoruba, a Nigerian tribe, at their religious ceremonies. They have been the sacred drums of Santeria in Cuba since the middle of the 16th century. This religion is based on ancient Yoruba rites from Nigeria, combined with elements of Catholicism.

In Cuba, the batá drum comes in three sizes. Each size has its own task. Played together, they serve to greet and accompany the Orishas, or deities. The smallest drum, called the "okókolo" (child), plays a number of basic rhythms, while the middle drum, called the "itótele" (father), and the large drum, "iyá" (mother), communicate in a rhythmic dialogue which is almost impossible to follow. The iyá is the most important member of a batá orchestra and is always played by an experienced musician. The iyá player sits in the middle, with the okónkolo on his right and the itótele player on his left. Only the mother drum has a series of bells on each side, and these sound when the bass tone is played.

Batás are traditionally made of wood, but now they are also made of fiberglass. The double conical shape of the drum consists of two halves connected together, so that a skin can be stretched across each end. The usual conga hardware is used for tightening the skin. A characteristic feature of the sound of the batá drum is the bright, wooden sound of the cha-cha (the smaller playing surface of the drum; see Imbaloke Rhythm on page 179).

Conga

There are actually three different types of conga, each with a different diameter and pitch. The quinto has the smallest diameter and highest pitch, while the tumba is the largest, with a deep pitch. The actual conga lies somewhere between the quinto and tumba in diameter and pitch. Because of the different sizes, the drums have different functions. For example, the tumba is used for playing bass parts, while the quinto and the conga usually play the solo parts or accompanying rhythms.

The quality of congas, which are mainly made of hardwoods—the wooden parts are cut to size and glued into a rounded shape—is very good nowadays. The same applies to fiberglass congas. The demand for a robust and extremely stable instrument brought about the revolutionary use of fiberglass panels and polyester resin for making congas. The head is usually made of untreated cowhide or the skin of a donkey. These natural skins, which must have a thickness of one sixteenth to one eighth of an inch, can be stretched tighter or loosened with a metal tensioning system. The solid tensioning ring lies about three eighths of an inch below the edge of the drum to prevent the hands from being injured. Riveted to the ring are at least five V-shaped pieces each of which holds an S-shaped tuning screw. Each screw goes through a tension block and is secured with a nut. The tension blocks are bolted to the drum and positioned below the counter hoop.

The skin can be tuned with a spanner. In order to stretch the skin correctly, you go from one tuning screw to the next in a clockwise direction and turn each screw just once, so that the pressure is evenly distributed; after playing the drum, you loosen the tuning screws in the same way to release the tension. This ensures that the skin can be used for a long time. From time to time the skin should be rubbed with some light oil, such as baby oil).

When you are working with a set of three congas, the intervals between the drums should be fourths, [11] though other intervals also have a certain charm. The basic techniques for playing this type of drum were further cultivated in Cuba, and developments in countries such as Columbia, Puerto Rico, etc. should not be overlooked, either. With the introduction of Afro-Cuban music in America in the 1940s by the legendary bongo player, Chano Pozo, the conga became a well-known instrument all over the world. Anyone interested in contemporary music will agree that the characteristic sound of this drum can be heard in many pop, funk, rhythm and blues, or jazz recordings. The conga is the best percussion instrument for the beginner. It is the center of any salsa combo and is the percussionist's most important instrument. (For playing techniques, see Part 5, page 151)

Bugarabu

Originating from Gambia and from the Casamance (southern Senegal), this drum is played at festivities and rituals in which the whole village takes part. Many songs are sung, with the purpose of resolving conflicts in the community. At these meetings a drummer plays on four drums that have a sound spectrum comparable to that of the congas, from the deep tumba up to the high quinto. The player's task is to drum the accompanying rhythms, as well as play solos. He is accompanied by women who play simple rhythmic basic patterns on pieces of wood.

---

[11]   For example, the lowest drum would be tuned to F, the middle to B, and the next to E flat.

The bugarabu comes in four sizes. It has a simple, varied tuning system. Handmade from the West African hardwood, win (see Djembé), the bugarabu is similar to the conga not only in its appearance and size, but also in the sound it produces. As its name indicates, the bugarabu, with its cowhide membrane, produces a warm, round sound. For the Djola people, it is the "sound of the heart of the Casamance." The rounded, singing tone seems to make your hands play on their own.

Atabaque

The atabaque is a long, wooden drum with African origins. It usually has a wedge tensioning system. The Brazilian atabaque comes in three models. The "le" is the smallest, the "rum" is the medium size, and the "rumpi" is the largest. Like the Cuban batá, the three atabaque form a single drum set which is used in the Candomblé ritual festivals in Brazil. When experienced musicians play the three drums together, they create rhythmical patterns (toques) dedicated to the Orishas (deities).

Atabaques are made with the traditional wooden barrel construction. A rope and wedge system or hardware is used to stretch the skin. The atabaque drumhead is characteristically smaller in diameter, in comparison with the Cuban conga. Atabaques are played with the hands, as well as with sticks. Because of their size, these drums can also be played while standing up.

Bongos

Bongos are two small single-skin drums of unequal size, which are joined together on a framework. The drums may be made of wood (like a barrel, of parts glued together), fiberglass or other synthetic materials. The Spanish name for the smaller, higher tuned drum is macho (man). The larger drum, which is more deeply tuned, is known as hembra (woman). The system for tuning these drums is similar to that used for congas (see page 32). However, there are no tensioning blocks; these are replaced by a tensioning ring, integrated into the bottom of the sound box. The bongocero (bongo player) holds the drums between his knees and usually plays them with his fingers, though they can also be played with thin timbale sticks. The bongo is a typical Cuban instrument, and next to the conga, it is probably the most widely played percussion instrument.

The most important basic rhythm for the bongos is the "martillo," which means "hammer" in Spanish. Bongos are perfect for playing rhythms such as the "Mambo," "Cha-Cha-Cha," or "Son Montuno."

Gonga

The gonga must be one of the most ingenious instruments in the world of drums. Gongas are made according to the traditional methods of construction. They have a striking, tapered, conical shape, with a sound box that is only about 10 inches long, and a resonator of the same length. This resonator, which can slide into the short body of the drum when traveling, in principle replaces the "missing" length of the sound box. A rubber ring on the inside of the plywood base plate enables the resonator to slide into the drum. The rubber ring also prevents the vibrating column of air which is produced during the drumming, from disappearing through the seam between the resonator and the sound box. The short body of the drum reflects the sound upward.

Despite its name, the sound of the gonga is nothing like that of the conga. Because of their modest size, three gongas are more or less the same weight as one large conga, and they fit together in a single conga bag. They can be arranged on a stand so that they can be played while sitting down or standing up.

Wood Drum

In contrast with the conga, where the tone is produced by the vibration of a stretched animal skin, the sound of the wood drum is produced by striking a thin wooden plate. The striking surfaces are made from finely grained wood 1/8th of an inch thick, covered with rosewood veneer, which gives the surface elasticity and durability. Even though it is made of wood, the sound plate reacts like a membrane, but it vibrates for a shorter period of time, resulting in the wood drum's characteristic sound.

Although the appearance of wood drums is clearly similar to that of congas, it would be wrong to describe them as "substitute congas." Particularly for beginners in this field, it should be pointed out that the different techniques used for playing the conga will only work with the wood drums when they have been fully mastered. Strokes such as the open stroke or slap stroke (see Playing Techniques for the Conga on page 151) can be used on wood drums without any problem, and with surprising results. The wood drums are about 30 inches tall and come in three sizes which fit one inside the other, like Russian dolls.

If you want to produce a different timbre on the wood drum, you can use mallets (beaters made of hard or soft rubber or felt). This produces the finest nuances, encompassing the entire range of sounds of wooden percussion instruments. With mallets, you can play on both the top and side surfaces of the wood drums.

Gome

The modern gome is also known as a table bass. It originates from West Africa, where it was one of the most original musical instruments. This extraordinary instrument, which is characterized by a penetrating full bass tone, is still part of the Ghanaian musical tradition, as it was in the past. When you go down to see the fishermen of the Ga tribe in the old town of Accra (Ghana), you will undoubtedly come across this musical instrument. It can be found in almost every highlife or gospel band, and is even used in traditional music.

It is believed that the gome bass was brought to Ghana from the Cameroons about 2000 years ago. In Ghana, the gome acquired a special significance for accompanying the songs about the suffering and suppression that the English invaders brought upon the Ga.

This drum's sound is created by a thin goat skin that is attached to the sound box with many small nails. The sound box of the gome consists of pieces of maple and alder, which are glued together to form an octagonal wooden frame. Inside this construction, there is a smaller wooden frame which is pressed against the skin with four long tap screws. These screws are in a wooden tensioning block, similar to that used in congas. When these tuning screws are turned inward, the inner wooden frame is pressed against the skin, and acts as a tensioning ring, making it possible to tune the bass drum. In Africa, small wooden wedges are also used to change the tone of the drum.

The bass drum is placed on the ground lengthways so that the player can sit on the broad side of the drum body and beat the skin with both hands from above, using the same techniques for playing the conga. In this position, the player can also change the tension of the skin with his heels.

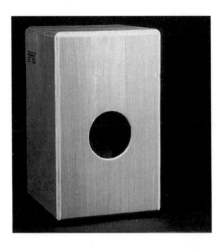

Cajon

The cajon (pronounced "cashon" or "cahon") comes from Latin America. In colonial times the slaves were forced to burn their drums, so they played on wooden boxes; this gave rise to the "rumba de cajon." As in the modern rumba (with its tumba, conga, and quinto congas), the rumba de cajon calls for three cajon drums of three different sizes. The rumba is not played during religious festivals, but is used at political and social events.

The modern form of the cajon (approximately 15' x 10' x 8') has two playing surfaces and is made of two sorts of wood. While the body consists of a light fir, both playing surfaces are made of rosewood veneer (1/32nd of an inch thick) which are glued together in five layers. The two sorts of wood in a single instrument produces a vibration with a very distinctive sound.

The cajon is held between the legs, and is played with the hands, or with a thick mallet. All the hand strokes of the conga technique can be used on the cajon without any problem. The cajon produces a sharp, penetrating sound with a rich range of tones.

The Cajon la Peru is a new model of the Cuban-Peruvian drum. When struck, it produces a distinctive, percussive rattling rises from the surfaces, along with a delicate bell-like sound that comes from the inside (where small brass bells are hanging on guitar strings that run across the instrument). A closer look reveals that the surface is partly attached with five tuning screws, in addition to being glued in the usual way. These screws can be tightened or loosened as required, allowing the player the ability to change the cajon's sound. Tightening the screws produces a tone with more bass, while less tension increases the sharp, rattling sound. The Cajon la Peru is further strengthened with reinforcing rods so that the player can sit down on it without any problem.

Udu

Udu drums are made of fired clay. The word "udu" means "bottle" in the Ido language. In Nigeria, where these drums originated, earthenware bottles, which had two openings, were found to produce this instrument's singular sound. In the past, the indigenous population believed that they could hear the sound of their ancestors in the udu drums. Since that time, these instruments have been used in religious ceremonies. This magical-sounding percussion instrument comes in different shapes and sizes. In addition to the standard models—udus with a high or deep tone—there is a double udu, and a small piccolo udu, so that a wide range of timbre can be realized with the udu.

To produce the udu's characteristic deep bass tone, you have to cover the openings on the side with the palm of your hand and then immediately open them again. This produces a warm bass tone with a timbre reminiscent of the Indian tabla. You can also play the udu with your fingers. There is also the "body sound" that further distinguishes this instrument. The longer the clay is fired, the higher the body sound. Lighter nuances can be produced which provide an attractive contrast with the deep bass sound. To produce a small change in pitch, the udu is filled with water or a special paste is applied in the opening at the top (the neck). When the udu drum is held between the legs, you can play it while sitting down, or you can use ring-shaped stands to play several drums with both hands.

Cuica

The cuica was originally an African instrument. This drum is rubbed, rather than beaten, and belongs to the friction instrument group. All friction drums have the common playing technique of is vibrating the membrane by rubbing it either with the fingers directly on the skin, or with a string or rod fixed in the membrane. There are drums like these in Europe, such as the foekepot. The cuica is played in a batucada (ensemble of samba instruments) during the Brazilian carnival.

A bamboo rod is fixed in the middle of the cuica's membrane. The characteristic cuica sound is produced by rubbing along this rod with a damp cloth in one hand while the middle finger of other hand changes the tone by pressing from the perimeter of the skin to the middle. The hand inside the cuica produces the hooting low tones, while the finger on the outside makes the suprising, high squeaks. In Brazil, there are cuica players who can play whole melodies on this instrument.

Cuicas come in different sizes, and the shape of the steel or brass sound boxes can be either conical or cylindrical. Large instruments with a thicker wall obviously produce a louder sound and can be heard more clearly in a large samba batucada. There are three decisive factors that determine the quality of the cuica's sound: first, the quality of the skin (a fine, even skin makes it more responsive), second, the thickness of the rod (a thin rod is better), and third, the number of tuning screws (the more tuning screws, the better the skin can be tuned).

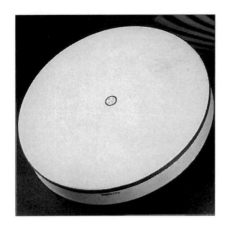

Frame Drum

This type of drum has a characteristically large diameter and a shallow body, which serves as a frame on which the skin is stretched. It comes from Arabia and North Africa. It requires a delicate finger technique.

Frame drums exist in various different sizes and types. The Irish bodhran (large) and the North African tar (medium) are well known examples of this range, each allowing for different possibilities because of their different shapes.

The instrument illustrated here, a modern version of the frame drum, is made of contemporary materials. A material called "acousticon"—a mixture of wood fiber and synthetic resin—is used for the frame. Acousticon is very durable, yet very light. Instead real leather, a synthetic, weatherproof material is used for the drumhead. As the original instruments were usually made with thin animal skins, they were strongly affected by moisture, so that they quickly went out of tune. The synthetic membrane of this frame drum is pre-tuned, and covered with a thin fiberglass layer on the back, so that, despite its large surface, it is evenly tuned.

Using the traditional playing technique, the frame drum produces a deep, warm sound in the bass range. On the other hand, the classic rim strokes produce a bright sound, which is very rich in harmonics.

Riq

The riq is an Arab hand drum, a simple instrument that can be played in many different ways. The history of this small frame drum goes back more than a thousand years. Made from an artistically decorated wooden frame, the riq is covered with fish or goat skin. The thin skin is glued to the frame to avoid the use of screws. Ten brass-colored pairs of rings are incorporated into the wooden frame, producing the typical sound of the riq. The diameter of the drum is about 10 inches. The frame has a width of about 2 inches.

This drum can be played in two different ways. In the simplest, most basic position, the riq is held upright between your left thumb and index finger, with your thumb pressed against a pair of bells and the skin facing away from your body. The characteristic way of playing this Arab tambourine consists of striking the bells with your right and left ring fingers, while your right index finger produces the traditional "dom" stroke on the skin, alternating with your right ring finger which does the "tak" stroke on the edge of the skin. In principle, this simple technique can be used to produce many interesting rhythms. The special effect created by the riq is achieved by the combination of the full dom strokes, the light rim strokes, and the clear sound of the bells.

Pandeiro

Probably the most popular Brazilian instrument, the pandeiro can be heard in the samba, as well as many other Brazilian rhythms. For example, it is played in the Capoeira (the ritual ceremony from Bahia), in the Forro, and the Frevo. This bell drum—which originally came from the Arab world, was brought to Portugal by the Moors, to finally end up in Brazil—has also received a great deal of attention in Western culture.

The pandeiro is a simple frame drum with narrow tin discs attached in pairs in the wooden ring. The shape of the discs give this instrument its characteristic sound; rounded discs produce a drier and rounder sound. To create a particularly dry sound, place a piece of corrugated cardboard between the wooden frame and the pairs of tin discs, so that the discs have less room to move. The pegs which hold the animal or synthetic skin on the frame are attached to simple tensioning blocks.

All the characteristic pandeiro strokes, like the thumb strokes, strokes with the ball of the hand, fingertips, and slaps produce interesting rhythms when they are combined in the right way. Anyone who would like to hear the sounds, or see the playing techniques of this instrument, should watch a performance or listen to a recording of the king of the pandeiro, the Brazilian, Airto Moreira.

Ocean Drum

This type of instrument is another sort of frame drum, but it is also undoubtedly the most extraordinary sound effect instrument, which can also be played as a drum. As soon as you hear it, it casts a spell on you with its amazingly accurate mimicry of the rushing sound of the ocean.

The impressive sound effect of the ocean drum belies its simple construction. The ocean drum (also known as the "surf maker") has specially developed synthetic membranes on both sides of the frame; one of these is transparent, so that you can see the small ball bearings inside the drum, waiting to roll across the skin to produce the rushing sound of the sea. The transparent skin allows the player to watch and control the rolling movement of the ball bearings.

The beautiful sound and strong dynamics of this percussion instrument speak for themselves. Equipped with pre-tuned skins, the ocean drum can also be played by striking it with an appropriate mallet, producing a marching drum sound.

Drums Played with Sticks

Doundoun

The bass drum or timpani of America and Europe finds its equivalent in the doundoun, which is a collective name for the kettle drums of Africa. This sort of bass drum is usually found as an accompanying instrument in djembé rhythms. The largest—the true doundoun—has a diameter of approximately 16 inches. The diameter of the sangban—the medium bass drum—measures approximately 12 inches. The kenkeni, the smallest of these drums, is the best known. Despite its diameter of only approximately 11 inches, it has a powerful sound. The names of these drums are onomatopoeic, imitating the sound of the instrument—a penetrating, warm bass tone—equally attractive in all three sizes.

These drums are made of very strong African hardwood with a striking brown color. When you see the large circumference of the doundoun, imagine how much time and patience it took to hollow out a tree trunk like this! The tensioning system consists of a thin iron ring covered with material with small loops, spaced 1-1/2 – 2-1/2 inches apart. A cord of synthetic material runs through these loops to hold the thick cowhide on each side of the drum firmly in place. A second ring is placed between the skin and the top tensioning ring, preventing the thick skin from shifting when it is tightened. A combination of different factors—such as the construction of the sound box from one piece of wood, the hardness of the wood, the thickness of the cowhide and the drum's overall large mass—affects the strength and warmth of the drum's impressive bass tone.

Bass drums are usually played with one stick. Traditionally, two or three drums are used in a set, and the right hand strikes the skins with a stick, while the left hand strikes an iron rod or iron bell attached to the body of the drum (also with a stick). Comparable to the technique used for playing the timbales, the drummer plays simple off-beat accents with the left hand, while playing basic patterns and their variations with the right hand. Some-times the bass drummer plays a solo in djembé music. But most of the time, the bass drummer serves as the heartbeat of the large djembé orchestra.

Talking Dum

While the art of writing has long been the most important means of long dis-tance communication in Western culture, in Africa the language of drums served this purpose. Drum language has the advantages of traveling faster than a messenger on horseback and communicating news to a larger number of people. In countries such as Ghana (where drum language is known as "donno," "dondo" or "dagomba"), Nigeria ("hausa"), Burkina Faso and Senegal ("tama"), this drum is used for that purpose. It originates from Nigeria, and has a special place in many ritual ceremonies.

The hour-glass-shaped sound box of the talking drum is made of African hardwood decorated with simple patterns, and has a drumhead on each end. There are extremely thin leather straps evenly space from each another, run-ning from one drumhead to the other, keeping the goatskins in place. Usual-ly a curved stick is used to beat on one of the membranes, but this drum can also be played with the hands.

The talking drum is perfect for expressing the seemingly incomprehensi-ble tonal language of Africa, because it not only produces the tones, but also glissandi. [12] To do this, you hold the instrument under your arm, so that when you press down firmly with your forearm on the straps running lengthwise, you increase the tension on the skins while beating on the drumhead. The higher the tension, the higher the tone. By tensing and relaxing very quickly, you can produce intriguing modulations of tone that seem like questions and answers ("Doo-wee?" "Wee-doo.").

---

[12]   'Glissandi' is plural for 'glissando,' which is a musical term indicating an almost seamless slide through a series of consecutive tones.

Surdo

The surdo is the largest drum in a bateria de samba, the percussion ensemble of samba schools. It is used as a bass drum, and is the central drum of the large percussion orchestra that moves through the streets of Rio de Janeiro during the carnival every year.

The drum hangs from the body by a belt so it can be played standing up or walking along. The traditional way of playing this drum consists of producing a muted tone, alternating with a ringing tone, with a surdo stick (a wooden stick with a round, wooden or felt head). The muted tone happens when the free hand rests on the skin while the other hand strikes with the surdo stick. This results in the typical surdo sound. Surdos have a cylindrical shape and are available in different sizes, from 14 x 24 inches to 24 x 26 inches. The sound box of the bass drum is made either of metal (aluminum or tin) or of wood.

In addition to synthetic skins, natural skins are also used, and are stretched on an aluminum or wooden frame. The skins can be tuned with the long tuning screws that run diagonally across the drum. In a samba orchestra, there are surdos of three different sizes. The largest surdo, the "marcacao," establishes the beat with its deep, resonating bass tone, while the smallest surdo, the "resposta," replies, as its name indicates. The tone interval between the two bass drums is a fourth. The "cortador" surdo (counter-surdo) is medium-sized and is used as a solo instrument connecting the other two with its rich rhythm variations. In samba schools— Escolas de Samba— up to 70 surdos play together.

Cylindrical drums with skins on each side are common throughout Latin America, and probably developed from the instruments played in former military bands. The zabumba is a flat bass drum from Brazil, and is used in baiao music, or in a forró rhythm. The drum has two skins and is played horizontally. As for the surdo, the system for tuning the drums consists of two tensioning rings which are connected by means of round iron rods, and these have hexagonal bolts at the end to tune the membranes. The "martelo"—a stick similar to that used with the surdo—is used with the right hand, while a thin wooden stick known as the "resposta" or "repique" is used with the left hand. The right hand drums the basic rhythm, while the left hand plays rhythmic counter strokes (or syncopated strokes) on the lower membrane. A more delicate sound can be produced if a piece of material is attached with cellophane to the groove or on the edge of the top membrane.

Repinique

The repinique is a typical Brazilian instrument which is mainly used in the classic samba batucada. The drum is struck with a thin wooden stick held in the right hand and produces a high-pitched tone. The left hand supports the repinique pattern with an off-beat rhythm. The way in which this drum is played—using sticks—is of African origin. The instrument itself is an adaptation of the European tin drum.

The striking feature of this drum is the wide cylindrical metal sound box, made of aluminum or steel. The two thin, synthetic membranes are stretched over the drum and are firmly tightened with eight to sixteen tuning pegs. Two tensioning rings keep the skins in place. Every part is coated with chrome. The sound of the repinique is characterized by a high, dry tone. The rim shots (striking the edge) produce a sharp percussive sound. In Brazil, the instrument is worn around the waist with a belt. The repinique player is responsible for conducting the Batucada, therefore certain repinique patterns introduce or conclude the playing of the samba orchestra. With the drum calls, the repinique player co-ordinates the progress of a "Bateria." The repinique is a fiery instrument and a favorite with every drummer who likes using drumsticks.

Caixa

The caixa, which means "box," is used in many Brazilian rhythms, such as the samba, frevo, maracatu, and baiao. Also known as the tarol, this flat, cylindrical, metal drum has membranes on each side, with snares stretched under the drum skin, making it a kind of snare drum, which can be used in drum traps as well as in marches. The only differences between the Brazilian and the European snare are the size and the finish of the drum. Many caixas used in the Escola de Samba are between 3 and 14 inches deep. They have a light aluminum or stainless steel construction, so that they can be carried easily. In Rio de Janeiro, many caixa players have several different snares stretched across the percussion surface to achieve a special sound for the street processions. The conventional technique of carrying the caixa is to attach it to a belt, so that the drum hangs in front of the stomach, and is not in the way when the drummer is walking. Other players prefer to carry the caixa on their shoulder, balancing it with the outstretched left arm; a position reminiscent of a violinist's. The drum, which usually has synthetic membranes, is struck with two sticks, using mainly rim shots, as well as pressed roll strokes (the stick is pressed on the skin). The characteristic drum patterns for the caixa are played in the samba in Balancado feeling (see Part 5, Samba Rhythm, on page 168).

Tambourim

This small frame drum, which usually has a single, tautly stretched skin, is a typical Brazilian percussion instrument and is used primarily in the large percussion orchestra of a samba batucada. This drum is also occasionally played in the "Capoeira de Angola" competition. The term "tambourim" is derived from the Portuguese word "tambor," which means "drum," and documents from as early as the first decade of the Portuguese colony in Brazil refer to this small drum.

The instrument is held in the left hand and played with a thin stick in the right hand. With the fingertips of the left hand resting on the inside of the skin, the player alternates between striking with the stick in the right hand and the middle finger of the left hand.

This hand drum is available in sizes from 5 to 8 inches in diameter and has a membrane made of animal skin or synthetic material. The frame is made of metal, wood, or plastic. Tambourims have tuning screws, so that, for example, when three or four tambourims are played together in a samba batucada, they can produce three or four notes. A great deal of tension on the membrane is necessary to produce this instrument's typical hard, penetrating sound, especially when the tambourims are used in the large "alas," the wing groups of the Escolas de Samba. Sambistas say that the role of the tambourim is *"dar a linha ritmica,"* which means that it provide a rhythmical guideline for the samba structure.

Tambora

Anyone who is interested in the tambora will inevitably come across the merengue, the most popular dance and musical form in the Dominican Republic. The typical merengue rhythm section includes instruments such as the metal or wooden guiro (see Part 3, page 71), and the tambora, which is played with a stick and the hand. The roots of the merengue lie in the music of the Bara tribe, who developed their forms of cultural expression on the island of Hispaniola (Haiti and the Dominican Republic). Toward the end of the last century, the merengue attained its classic style. The guitar, which had commonly been used up to that time, was replaced by the accordion, and percussion instruments were added. Since then, the sharp sound of the metal guiro and the tambora have determined the characteristic sound of the merengue.

There are many variations in the way the tambora is played. Despite its simple structure, it has unlimited potential to provide a rich variety of sounds for the off-beat of a rhythm. Usually, the player sits with the drum held in his or her lap. A belt, strapped around the thighs, keeps the drum in place. When standing, the player can position the belt to carry the drum in front. The right hand beats on the right membrane with a drumstick, producing open or muted tones. For the basic rhythm, wooden "clack" sounds are important; these are produced on the tensioning ring or on the sound box. The left hand completes the rhythm, usually with slaps or open tones. However, other conga techniques can also be used, using the ball of the hand and the fingertips.

The traditional tamboras in Santo Domingo and Puerto Rico are still made of hollowed-out tree trunks, and a medieval rope system keeps the skins tight. Modern tamboras are built on a construction principle similar to that of the wooden conga. Wooden sections are glued together with great precision to make a round barrel, and modern hardware replaces the old rope tensioning system. In addition, a wooden block is added to the sound box and tensioning ring of the tambora illustrated here, to help withstand instense drumstick use.

Timbales

The timbales are a traditional instrument in salsa music. They consist of two metal drums (steel or brass), which usually have synthetic membranes, and are mounted together on a stand. The sounds of a set of timbales include those of the cha-cha bell, a mambo bell, and sometimes a cymbal. The drums are played with the hands and with sticks that are noticeably thinner than traditional drumsticks. The tone interval between the large and the small drum lies between a third and a fifth. The drums come in different sizes, ranging from small timbalitos to the large timbalon (also known as "thunder timbales") used in Latin American big bands because of its big sound. The diameter of the drums in these bands goes up to 15 or 16 inches, compared to the standard size of 13 and 14 inches. Timbalitos start at 8 inches. The "paila" technique, in which certain rhythms (cascaras) are played on the right and left side of the sound box, is commonly used playing style for the timbales.

Steel Drum

The steel drum comes from the Caribbean. However, the models illustrated here were made by a German instrument maker, using old oil drums. The

different tones produced on the surface of the drums are related to its striking, concave shape. With a felt-tip marker, you can drawn letters on the different indented areas to indicate the pitch produced there, to make it easier to
find the right tone when playing a particular melody. The small holes drilled
in some steel drums around separate tonal areas are not decorative, but help
produce a tinnier, soft sound. The classical steel drum does not have these
holes, and has a crystal-clear sound.

It is possible to play countless melodies with two pencil-sized drumsticks with round rubber heads, which are used extremely sensitively to produce a delicate, charming effect. When steel drums are tuned pentatonical-
ly, [13] every tone that is produced is harmonious. People without any musical
knowledge can easily discover their own sound patterns on this instrument.
There are also steel drums with a chromatic scale, in which the placement of
the twelve notes is determined by the system of the circle of fifths.

Sakara

The sakara is a small frame drum from Liberia and Nigeria. It consists of a
small ring of fired clay, which is covered with a thin goatskin. When the skin
is stretched on the frame, the overlapping part is attached with small, sharp
wooden or bamboo pegs, in such a way that the tension of the skin is maintained when it is dry. Sakaras are slightly reminiscent of Brazilian tam-
borims, but have a deeper and warmer sound.

The African sakara is played with a curved stick. The drum should be
held in the left hand so that your thumb is below the clay edge of the drum
and the fingers are on the drum skin. In this way, you play soft fingertips
strokes with your fingers, while the curved stick beats the main rhythm. As

---

[13]   Using only five tones, usually the first, second, third, fifth, and sixth tones of a diatonic
scale, i.e. using the diatonic C scale, the pentatonically-tuned steel drum would have areas
tuned to C, D, E, G, and A. Chromatic steel drums have twelve distinct tones.

the animal skin is very sensitive to moisture, it is important to keep the drum somewhere dry.

Shaman Drums

The frame drum shown here, like the thunder drum shown below, is often known as a shaman drum, because this drum, with membranes on one or two surfaces, is used particularly in shamanic ritual. In this tradition, the membrane of the drum is viewed as the "spiritual horse," which transports the shaman to all sorts of areas of consciousness. Some shaman drums come from Asia, but the drums illustrated here come from the Native American Indian culture, and are therefore also known as Indian drums. The shape of the kettle drum is based on a cylindrical wooden sound box; the barrel is made of a single piece of wood and comes in different sizes. The drums made by the Pueblo Indians are based on the same traditions and made with the same care as they were centuries ago. They are made of different sorts of local wood, such as the wood of the poplar tree, and the hide of a moose or buffalo. The wood is stored for a year before it is used. No special system is used to stretch the skin over the drum. The skins are kept in place with thick leather straps. The natural sound of these drums has a magical effect on the listener. They are played with drumsticks, and occasionally with the hands. Pueblo Indians use these simply-designed instruments in their cultural and religious ceremonies.

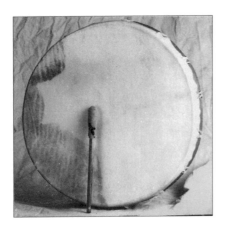

Thunder Drum

This exotic drum originates from India, and its effective sound explains its name. The shape is reminiscent of a traditional frame drum, but the thunder drum is made in different sizes. The broad wooden frame is made of hard oak, and the membrane is made of horse skin. Amazingly, no screws or nails are used for securing the frame, or for stretching the membrane. Traditionally, the skin was stretched by long, thick leather straps, knotted together to form a cross, which also served as a handle. A soft felt beater is used to produce thundering drum sounds on this instrument.

The thunder drum was originally an instrument used by the shamans (see shaman drum). It is also used in "sun dance" rituals. As a handmade instrument, the thunder drum is very sensitive to heat and moisture. If the drum produces an irregular tone, it is possible to carefully adjust the tension of the skin with a natural or artificial source of heat.

Buk, Daiko

The buk, which comes from Southeast Asia, is a so-called barrel drum with membranes stretched on each side (illustration right). In Japan this drum is known as the daiko. The largest of these is known as the O-daiko. This is a drum used in Shinto temples. These drums are made from a wooden tree trunk which is hollowed out by hand, and can range from small instruments (shime-daiko) to enormous instruments. The instrument maker stretches skins across the sound box, and these are usually nailed down. The history of this type of drum begins in China, and from there passed to Southeast Asia via the Zen monasteries of Korea and Japan. The buk, the daiko, and the O-daiko are usually played standing up, with two drumsticks. The sound produced by these drums is warm and voluminous.

On the island of Sado, on the west coast of Honshu, a group of Japanese drummers are working in accordance with the tradition of daiko drumming. This group is called Kodo, which means heartbeat, as well as "the children of the drum." Their drum music has an incredible intensity and power (see Discography on page 193).

Godrum

The powerful, mighty sound of the godrum will enchant any listener. Low frequencies and many semitones are characteristic of this Asian gong drum. The membranes on each side allow two or more drummers to produce a rhythmic alternation. The timbre can be changed by using different drumsticks. The godrum has a diameter of 35 inches and is 12 inches wide. It produces an intense sound and has an attractive appearance (see illustration).

Split Drum

Split drums, which are known all over the world, are among the oldest instruments, and were some of the first drums used for sending messages. There are small instruments, as well as very large ones such as the gigantic split drums from Assam. These consist of tree trunks which have been carefully hollowed out, leaving only a cylinder. The slit on the top creates two "sound tongues" which produce different tones because of their varying thickness. There are different types of split drum, but those with a simple straight split are the most commonly-used for sending messages. Split drums vary from simple to ornate instruments decorated with wood carvings, and they are played with either drumsticks or the hands. The messages played on split drums are almost always coded, and consist of a series of phrases which correspond to comparable events, e.g., the arrival of a white man or a policeman.

Inspired by the traditional construction, a whole new generation of split drums developed, with an attractive appearance and beautiful sound (see big bom). The split drum is available in various sizes and has a resonating lid made of wood or aluminum. Four to six sounding slits, which are precisely cut in the surface lid, determine the open tuning. This produces an instrument which is between a drum and a xylophone because of its atonal sound spectrum; this is the instrument's special charm.

Played with two mallets (with hard rubber or felt heads), this drum is reminiscent of the archetypal sounds of African and South American music. It is also easy to play with the fingers. The best sound is produced by striking the middle of the tongues. The split drum is widely used in music education.

Big Bom

The appearance of this extremely large split drum is as fascinating as its very special spectrum of deep sounds.

The sound box for the big bom is not made of a thick tree trunk like the traditional split drum; the resonating body consists of plates of fir, about of an inch thick. The cover has eleven thick, long sound tongues, made of very hard and heavy American maple. When played with felt beaters, these tongues produce a deep, warm sound. The pattern of grooves on the cover is like an Indian tree of life, slightly changed so that the range of sounds can be used to optimum effect. The spectrum of tones of the open, tuned sound tongues cannot be clearly determined, which is part of this instrument's musical appeal.

Water Drum

The water drum is found predominantly among the Malinke and Senufo tribes. The territory of the Senufo tribe stretches across three African states: Mali, the Upper Volta, and the Ivory Coast. In contrast with hide-covered drums which are played exclusively by men in Africa, the water drum is played primarily by women. The words, "Gi dunu," which are used for this drum by the Senufo, give an indication of the sound it makes.

This unusual African drum usually consists of the skin of a hard gourd filled with water, and a smaller one which floats on the water with the rounded side up. In Africa, these are struck by two narrow, spoon-shaped gourds. The usual drum set consists of two water drums. The instruments are tuned in fourths and are played by female musicians who belong to the "Poro," a community of women who have high social and religious standing.

Using plastic bowls—which are on sale in every size—to hold the water, several gourds can be floated on the water to serve as sounding boxes. This is a good arrangement because the plastic bowl is much stronger for holding water than the skin of a gourd, and a real melody can be achieved with a series of four to six water drums of different sizes. The pitch is determined primarily by the diameter of the floating gourd. However, the gourds can also be more finely tuned by submerging them deeper in the water. The sound produced is unusually round, accompanied by bright nuances. The larger the volume of water in the container, the more powerful and fuller the sound of the "underwater bass." It is a good idea to play this drum with rubber or felt beaters; these make the warm sound of the water drum come better into its own.

Table Drum

The pentagonal table drum (with a diameter of three feet and over), which is used for therapeutic purposes, is a very special type of drum. It was invented by the American music therapists, B. Bernstein and Dr. A. Clair, and is aimed above all at people suffering from dementia. The deep frequencies from this drum lie below the hearing level, but can still be detected. Strong vibrations are produced by the extremely large vibrating surface; these are mainly detected in the lower half of the body when you sit down at the table drum. Several people at the same time can play this drum, either with their hands or with beaters.

Part 3

Other Sounding Instruments

Idiophones

The term "idiophone" is used for instruments that produce their sounds by means of membranes (skins), columns of air, or strings that vibrate in all sorts of different ways. Some people experience the sound as unpleasant or disruptive, yet enticing.

The development of sounding instruments started from the time when primitive people noticed that hitting together two stones, bones, or sticks produced sounds. The sound of the voice was accompanied by clapping, the dull sound of stamping feet, and the sounds of countless primitive, natural instruments, which are still used in many cultures today.

Many sounding instruments have a particular quality in which the relationship between the harmonics is often distorted, and resonates in a medium to high frequency spectrum. This is usually described as a rushing or rustling sound, or simply as noise, rather than music. An example of this sound quality and its effect is the rattle, which—along with the drum and the didgeridoo—is one of the oldest instruments. The clear, refreshing sound of the rattle makes a vital impression as a sacred instrument used in ceremonies and initiation rituals.

The French ear specialist, Dr. A. Tomatis, showed that the ear is involved in supplying approximately 90% of the energy received by the cerebral cortex. This stimulation is caused primarily by high frequencies and can increase vitality, concentration, and mental clarity. We can become charged up by the high frequencies of melodic instruments, and this prevents us from becoming tired when we dance.

The gong, with its enormous spectrum of frequencies, has comparable energizing properties. There are gongs that produce vibrations with a very high frequency, and gongs that produce sound waves with a low frequency; they each have a different influence. When gongs are played within a broad spectrum of harmonic vibrations, one is confronted with the gong's psychoactive sound fields, which can be an either stimulating or relaxing physical experience. The sound patterns of a gong can evoke different associations, just like other instruments that produce sound effects and rushing sounds, such as the ocean drum, the rainmaker, the chimes and the didgeridoo. These instruments' evocative powers make them extremely important in music therapy, apart from their general musical application.

There are many different types of idiophones. The most common are: shaking instruments, percussion instruments, scraping instruments, bells, sticks, cymbals and gongs; this list immediately shows the different ways in which the instruments produce sounds. Idiophonic playing techniques include shaking, as with the ganza from Brazil, striking, as in the case of the gong and mallet, scraping, as with the Cuban guiro, plucking, as with the kalimba, or hitting together, as with claves.

The sounding instruments presented here are among the most commonly found and are heard in many genres of modern music. They are usually made of wood or metal. In the modern technological age, the possibilities of synthetic materials have also been harnessed to make exotic percussion instruments. The key material is fiberglass, which is light and extremely durable. Fiberglass, which was first used to make congas, is now the basic material for a large number of sounding instruments.

The ancient world of sounding instruments, which I have divided into five groups in this book, is extremely diverse. In an attempt to produce ever different and new sounds, the music industry has developed some interesting new instruments. There are many different percussion instruments with familiar, usual, and unusual timbres, but this book cannot contain them all, so I have had to make a choice. A number of the instruments I have chosen—the didgeridoo and some variations on the flute—are not strictly idiophones, and sometimes not even percussion instruments, because the way they are played is based on different principles. However, they have been included in this book because they are popular as sound effect instruments within the percussion group.

These sound effect instruments, gongs and sound discs, as well as other instruments, are commonly heard in film or meditation music, in therapeutic music forms, as well as in a well-rounded percussionist's repertoire of instruments. I hope some of the tips on holding and playing these instruments will encourage you to have a go youself!

Percussion Instruments

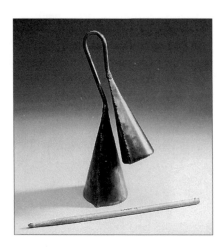

**African and Brazilian
Double Bells**

The double bells, which are idiophones, are used in various different musical styles in Africa and Brazil. Two funnel-shaped metal bells connected at the narrow end give this instrument a rather exotic appearance.

Bells have an important function in the structure of African and Brazilian music. The rhythmic patterns that are played on the double bells have been described as a time-line formula, guideline or clave. Bells give rhythmically support the musicians in a group, serving, like claves (sounding bars), as a metronomic backbone. The clear sound of bells and claves is ideally suited for creating a contrast against the more complex rhythm patterns of drums, so that the essential rhythmic foundations become unambiguously audible. A typical pattern for the bell used in both Africa and Brazil is the 12/8 or 6/8 clave (see Part 4, page 141).

The African style bell in the photograph is a modern representation of the double African bell. Like the African example, it contains two funnel-shaped bells of different sizes, but in this case they are not made of iron, but of thin tin. A narrow piece of metal, joining the tops of the two bells, provides firm support.

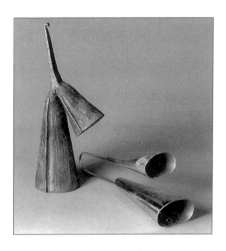

Agogo
Gonkogui

Black iron bells are predominantly played in African music, in places such as Togo, the Cameroons, Nigeria, and the Congo. The double bells shown on the right owe their name to the Yorubas. They were taken to the Caribbean and Brazil by the Bantus (who call the instrument "ngonge," which means "time and respect"), and the Yorubas (who call it "agogo"), as part of their African culture. The agogo is used in the Brazilian Candomblé rituals, as well as in Brazilian street samba. This bell is characterized by a clear, bright sound, rich in harmonics, and is usually tuned in intervals of a third, fourth or fifth. It comes in many different versions. The clicking sounds you often hear in Brazilian music are made by briefly pressing the bells together with the left hand. The handle acts as a spring so that the bells return to their original position.

One of the most interesting African double bells comes from Ghana, where it is known as "gonkogui." (on the left in the illustration). When struck with a stick, it sounds like cowbells. Played with a mallet, it produces softer, warmer, and rounder tones. A special sound effect can be achieved by holding the bells so that the mouth of the larger bell is pointed toward your stomach. You then strike the bell with a wooden stick and immediately press the opening against your stomach so that the sound softly fades away. It takes some practice, but eventually leads to interesting and attractive sound patterns (e.g., see Part 5, Gamamla, on page 174).

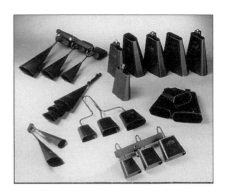

Cowbells/Tribells/Combibels

A great deal of attention has been paid in recent years to interesting sounding bells, and a new generation of metal bells has developed: cowbells, tribells, agogo bells and combibells. These include the common metal bells used in Latin American salsa and Brazilian music; the cha-cha, the handbell (campana), the timbales, the mambo bells, the fusion bell, and the chico bell. All the bells, except for the chico bell, are available in two styles. One style is based on the example of the classic cowbell, with flat playing surfaces for the body of the bell. The other style has a small curve in the middle of both percussion surfaces.

The handbell, which is also known by the name bongo bell or campana, exists in high-toned model, such as the hand rock bell, and in a deep-toned model, such as the Latin salsa handbell. In a tonal classification, the chico, cha-cha, and fusion bells produce a high to middle range of tones, while the mambo, timbales, and handbell cover a spectrum of deeper tones.

All the cowbells, with the exception of the handbells, are fully welded and can be attached to the timbales or a drum kit. A cowbell has two sound characteristics. First, in principle, a cowbell should have a dry sound without being too dull. Second, the upper range should be balanced and free of unpleasant frequency modulations. The cowbell sound is powerful and metallic.

In addition to angular bells, there are bells that are funnel-shaped, like the agogos of the Brazilian street samba bands. Apart from the hand-held agogos and the mounted agogo, there are also the tritone and combibells, which produce a harmonious scale of three tones. The tritone agogo bell has an exceptional construction; three funnel-shaped bells are arranged in such a way that they appear to be all in one. The mounted tritone agogo bell has three funnels of bells mounted next to each other on a metal strip.

The combibell, the hand tritone and the mounted tritone agogo bell are made into a set of bells that produces six tones. With its attachment screw, this model, like all the other mounted versions, can also be added to a percussion or drum kit. This set of bells gives the drummer a wide range of musical possibilities, because of the tuned metal bells' broad spectrum of tones.

The ridge rider rock cowbell is a completely new creation in the cowbell range. The special feature of this cowbell is the piece of plastic next to the sound hole. It serves as a mute, making it unnecessary to use cellophane tape on the cowbell to reduce irritating harmonics, as many percussionists have done in the past.

Woodbells

The creator of this instrument has clearly proven that it is possible to make bells of wood. Wooden bells, which are popular in music therapy and education, comprise a range of sophisticated percussion instruments. In order to achieve a full sound, oak is used for the surfaces of the bells. The two holes in the bells allow them to be attached to a special base, in an arbitrary order, and tuned in different keys. These wooden bells have been tuned in a pentatonic scale and have a warm, penetrating sound when struck with hard rubber beaters. Felt beaters make the sound softer. A hard wooden stick is not suitable, for the wood bell, as the instrument would lose its round, percussive sound.

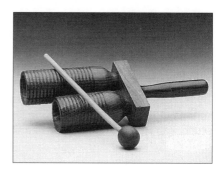

Wooden Agogo

The wooden agogo, which is sometimes heard on recordings of samba music, reveals its musical possibilities in Candomblé, the traditional Brazilian music of the gods. The version pictured here is made of American hardwood, but was inspired by the metal agogo. Two long wooden tubes of different lengths serve as the sounding body. They are firmly glued onto a narrow wooden frame with a sturdy wooden handle. The outside of the tubes is corrugated, giving the bell its characteristic warm sound when it is struck softly with a wooden stick. The corrugation also allows the player to use the wooden agogo like a guiro (see the following description). The instrument can be scraped to produce a high or deep spectrum of tones. Because of the combination of delicate scraping sounds and the short wooden sounds made by striking the wood, the agogo can be considered a sound effect instrument.

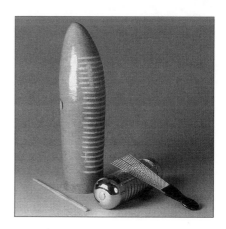

Guiro

Anyone who is involved with Cuban percussion music knows that the guiro is an essential instrument in salsa music, and it is also used to accompany the cha-cha-cha. Based on the original Cuban construction, the guiro is made from a hollowed-out gourd. As on the reco-reco (see page 78), there are regularly-spaced indentations on the gourd's surface. The sound of the guiro comes into its own when you play it as follows: the instrument is held vertically in the left hand so that the thumb and the index finger hold the holes at the bottom, and a thin wooden stick is scraped over the indentations in a movement parallel to the instrument.

A professional guiro looks just like the original, but is made of thin fiberglass. Because fiberglass is extremely hard without being dense, this instrument can produce a very loud sound. It contains two holes in the back for holding it, and two additional patterns of indentations for producing different effects. There are also metal guiros, which are played with a comb-shaped, metal scraper. As the metal guiro is mainly used in merengue music, it is also known as the merengue guiro.

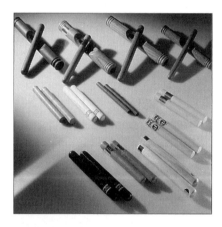

Claves

These round wooden bars are the most characteristic instruments in Latin American music. They are easy to play. One wooden bar is held in the middle, between your thumb, the base of your thumb and your fingertips, so that the cupped palm of your hand forms a resonating chamber under the wood. Despite their simple construction, it is surprising how diverse the design and sound of claves are nowadays, as is clear from the photograph below. The use of fiberglass, among other materials, has resulted in new developments. Fiberglass claves have an extremely robust construction. They are unbreakable and are slightly heavier, so they can be played very loudly. These claves are particularly suitable for loud salsa big bands, or for pop and rock groups, which are increasingly using claves nowadays.

Meanwhile, there have also been further developments of the standard versions, for example, of African claves. These differ from the classical model in size and finish. In contrast with the older versions, the round piece of wood is longer and broader with simple wooden designs at each end. Additional resonance is produced by drilling a hole through the middle of the wood and shaving out an area the size of a hand in the middle of the sounding box. This gives the African claves a deeper, fuller timbre. In one special version of the claves, the conventional shape of the wood has been replaced by a flatter, broader shape. There are shallow indentations along the length of the piece of wood which makes it easier to hold and allows for different percussive possibilities. Anyone who has seen the group Kodo will know how these Asians use the claves.

Woodblock

These simple wooden percussive instruments are certainly among the oldest in the world. Nowadays, the woodblock is used in music education, as well as in orchestral pieces, and is also often part of the equipment of a multi-percussionist. The woodblock is constructed of different hardwoods glued together in a solid block, giving it great percussive dynamics and stability.

Woodblocks produce a wooden, percussive sound. When a hard beater is used, the woodblock produces its characteristic, sharp, penetrating sound. Woodblocks are available singly or in sets of three, which are tuned to different pitches, and they come with a metal stand, to which they can be easily attached.

Jamblock

The jamblock is actually a revolutionary type of woodblock. It is made of a new type of extremely strong synthetic material known as Jeniger, which makes the jamblock sound all the more astonishing. When the jamblock is struck with an ordinary wooden stick, it produces a lovely sound of natural wood with a sharp edge. The secret of this sound lies in the shape of the instrument. Its futuristic design distinguishes the appearance and the warm timbre. The raised percussive surface, rather like a swollen lip, makes that it easy to play. The jamblock can be quickly assembled, with three pre-drilled holes, to a steel frame. It is available in a low- and high-pitched versions, and is a popular instrument with percussionists.

Longophone

The longophone is one of the many contemporary types of xylophone, yet it is based on the authentic forms found, for example, in Africa, where xylophones have fulfilled an important function in folklore in ceremonial music for many generations. In general, a xylophone consists of a row of wooden bars of various lengths, which are sounded with two sticks. Different methods are used to amplify this sound. For example, there are trough and resonating xylophones. They are tuned to the old pentatonic scale, like the Orff xylophone. Possibly the best known African xylophone is the balaphone, for which gourds are used as resonators under the sounding bars. In the Amadinda culture, there are xylophones that are played by several musicians at the same time.

The large longophone in the photograph is a contemporary example of one of these group instruments. The players must sit opposite each other and strike the rounded ends of the ash sounding bars with round sticks similar to claves. This produces a penetrating wooden sound and encourages endless experimenting and improvising with the sounding bars. The melody and rhythm intermingle to form a single pattern of sound. Different scales can be used, such as the completely chromatic scale, or ethno scales, which are chosen by the individual players. This leads to all sorts of interesting possibilities in contemporary percussion music and other styles, as well as in music therapy.

Temple Block

Looking at the shape of this instrument, it is clear why it is known in Korea by the name "wooden fish." The temple block is carved from camphor wood. It has a large, striking handle, and is covered with a transparent layer of varnish. A warm, deep wooden sound is produced by striking the curved wood with a wooden stick or a rubber or felt beater. In Japan, the instrument is known as "mu yü." In Buddhist meditation exercises, the wooden fish is used as an independent instrument to indicate the meter. It is struck with a thick wooden rod and accompanies singing, as well as indicating changes in tempo in the ceremony.

Since musicians in the West discovered this exotic percussion instrument, its playing method and musical possibilities have changed. Because it is available in many different sizes, it is possible, with a line of five temple blocks, to produce melodies as well as percussive music.

This beautiful wooden instrument is widely used in various forms of contemporary music. Single instruments are usually used in therapeutic rhythm exercises.

Wooden Clap

This Indian instrument was rediscovered in the search for something new. The wooden clap consists of six plywood strips of varying thickness, 27 inches long, which are glued together at one end to form a handle. You hold the wooden clap one hand so that your thumb is placed firmly on the flat handle. You move it quickly up and down so that the thin strips strike against each other. If you wish to achieve a shorter clapping effect, move your hand to move the middle of the instrument so that the strips of wood cannot vibrate as much. You can get a staccato clap by holding the wooden clap the right hand and hitting it against the left palm. You can also play interesting rhythmic patterns with the use of two wooden claps.

Devil Chase

The devil chase lives up to its name: the sound of this 16-inch long percussion instrument from the Philippines is anything but angelic. The apparent simplicity of the instrument makes the extraordinary sounds that it produces all the more surprising. The devil chase is an exotic member of the family of percussion instruments, and will challenge any musician who comes into contact with it for the first time. And yet it is fairly simple. The instrument is made of a piece of bamboo, split length-wise, so that there are two sounding tongues. By lightly striking one of these sounding tongues against a soft background such as the palm of your hand, the two halves of the bamboo start to vibrate. This results in a humming, sometimes buzzing, and sometimes roaring sound. There is a small opening at the end of the bamboo tube. If you open and close the opening with the thumb of the right hand, you can influence the vibration of air in the strip and change the pitch of the sound. As each devil chase is made individually, the timbre and intensity of the sound differs from instrument to instrument.

Reco-Reco

The sound produced by the reco-reco evokes associations with animal or jungle noises. The sound is achieved by scraping the instrument's uneven surface. Scrapers such as this were known both in Pre-Columbian times and in Africa. As far as we know, the Aztecs and their contemporaries made these instruments with bones that had been hollowed out at certain intervals so that they could be scraped with a second, thinner bone. The reco-reco is also available in a bamboo version and a metal version. In the latter, several metal springs are stretched over the resonating body of the instrument.

To play this instrument, you hold it horizontally in one hand, while moving a thin, round, wooden or metal stick—held in your right hand at a right angle to the instrument—along the length of the tube.

The reco-reco is used mainly in Latin America and Brazil, and, above all, plays an important role in samba and related musical genres. It is a good idea for you to experiment with wooden sticks of different lengths and thickness; these produce very effective sounds.

Snail

The snail is a very unusual percussion instrument that is particularly suitable for special effects. It is hand-wrought entirely of metal, and consists of a flat, drum-shaped sound box, with a flattened bell welded to it, and a spring stretched between two welded hooks. This spiral can be played like a reco-reco, and it produces a striking resonating sound when the sound box and bell are played. Attached to the middle of the sound box is a sounding bracket. When struck with a wooden stick, the bracket produces a bright, clear tone, rich in harmonics. The strange construction of the instrument allows for many different timbres, and the metal spring ensures that the sound resonates with a distinct rushing effect. The instrument can be held in the hand, or mounted on a stand.

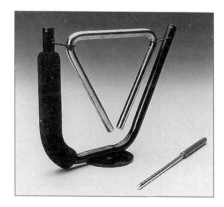

Trigger-triangle

The triangle, with its delicate, clear sound, is a popular instrument in both European and Brazilian musical styles. The word "trigger" indicates that the instrument is a percussion instrument in the truest sense of the word. The classical triangle has to be held up, or at least suspended in such a way that it does not touch anything anywhere, but the trigger triangle is built so that it can be placed and played anywhere. It is suspended from two rubber rings in a U-shaped frame with a base plate. For more complicated rhythms with open and muted strokes, the frame has a foam handle, so that it is easy to pick up and mute the sound, as required, with the same hand.

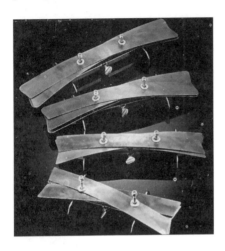

Crasher

The sound of this instrument is a result of its remarkable construction. A closer look reveals that the crasher consists of three thick metal plates which are loosely threaded onto two metal bolts. The metal strips are about 10 inches long and slightly curved. This curved shape ensures that the strips spring up when they are struck, so that they clatter as much as possible.

You play this instrument with a wooden stick and you can either attach it to a cymbal stand or hold it in the palm of your hand. Because the crasher's strips can be made in different widths, it gives you a choice between four patterns of sound, in addition to its unusual, rushing effect. The crasher is very suitable for producing a quick, hissing sound.

Crash Box

The perfect instrument for drummers and percussionists, the crash box produces an unusual and very attractive sound. With the appropriate mallets on the five sounding surfaces—each with a different pitch—the crash box produces distinct, bright, rattling sounds. If you listen carefully, you'll recognize that the sound is reminiscent of the African balaphone. The wooden body, divided into five sound boxes, is made of veneered plywood. Each of the five resonating chambers has a hole in the bottom. Very fine plywood is used for the surface of this percussion instrument. Only one side of the surface is glued to the body, so that the plywood plate can vibrate slightly. You can simply placed the crash box on the ground or attache it to a swivel stand. The hard rubber mallets that are used for the vibraphone are also suitable for the crash box, and they produce a bright sound. When played with a soft mallet, the crash box produces a warmer sound with more bass.

Shaking Instruments

Maracas

Native peoples consider rattles to be among the most important accompanying instruments. Even today, shamans know about the special effects of the sound, and use them in their rituals, often in combination with song.

In South America, rattles are known as maracas. They belong to the group of shaking idiophones, and are essential in the large range of the percussionist's repertoire of instruments.

Maracas are prominent in rhythms such as the mambo, cha-cha-cha or caboclinhos. Therefore, the name "samba balls," which they are sometimes called, is not entirely accurate. Maracas are usually made of hollowed-out gourds with a round or oval shape. Each gourd is filled with seeds, small pebbles and so on, and has a wooden handle. When shaken correctly, it rattles.

As music constantly develops, so do the instruments themselves. For example, the maracas used in early salsa music often had sound boxes made of skin. Two to four damp pieces of skin cut to size were stretched over a round bottle and stitched. When the skins dried, the bottle was removed, leaving the outline in the hard leather. These maracas can still be found today, and produce a very dry, full sound that appeals to many musicians because it perfectly accompanies the congas, bongos and timbales. Nowadays, there are also maracas made of indestructible synthetic materials. One manufacturer has improved maracas even further by making it possible to change the filling, and therefore the timbre. The handles can be removed and the filling can be added to, reduced or even replaced altogether, so that all sorts of sounds can be produced. In this way, the maracas can be adapted for any special requirements.

Caxixi

The caxixi was originally played by a berimbau player (see berimbão on page 116). However, musicians like Airto Moreira have broken away from the traditional playing methods and have started to develop new techniques.

The caxixi is a plaited basket with a handle. The base consists of a piece of curved gourd, and the instrument is filled with small seeds. A caxixi makes various patterns of sound, depending on how you use it. You hold in the right hand so that the bottom of the gourd faces down. If you move the caxixi to the left and down, so that the filling hits the base of the gourd, you'll get a sharp, dry sound. If you move the instrument quickly to the right and up, the seeds strike the basketwork at the top and a softer sound is produced. By moving it in different ways, the two sounds can be combined to make many rhythmic patterns.

There is also a more modern version of this instrument. It has a fiberglass bottom instead of a gourd, and a filling consisting of plastic beads that produce a considerably sharper sound.

Chicken Shake

"Chicken shake" is and amusingly appropriate name for these colorful plastic eggs filled with small ball-bearings. This fairly new instrument comes in four colors, each indicating a different amount of filling, the amount of which determines the fine nuances in the sound. For example, the Chicago Blue chicken shake has the largest quantity of small balls and therefore produces a dense, full sound. The Mellow Yellow chicken shake, on the other hand, contains the smallest amount of this fine rattling material and therefore sounds brighter and more open. All the chicken shakes have an unusually clear and subtle sound. These small percussion instruments produce a great effect. In technical terms, they are played in the same way as the Brazilian ganza. Varying patterns of sounds can be produced by holding the chicken shake in different ways. By holding the plastic egg between the thumb and the palm of your hand so that, when you shake it, your other fingers alternately grasp and let go of the egg, you can suppress the sharp extremes of sound and produce a more muted sound.

Shékere

The shékere consists of a dry, hollowed-out gourd covered with a network of plastic beads. Traditionally the nets were made in Cuba using large seeds which produced a softer sound. The modern shékeres covered with synthetic beads create a more penetrating sound. The shape—round, or more elongated—and the size of the gourd also influence the sound produced by the instrument. The network of beads sets the rhythm, and should move evenly to and fro to the beat of the music.(For a detailed explanation of techniques for playing the shékere, see Part 5, page 157.)

The shékere is used in many musical styles in Cuba. The guiro (a musical style that comes from the Nigerian Yorubas, not to be confused with the instrument of that name) can be played on three shékeres with different pitches. In African and Brazilian music, the shékere also provides the rhythm for many percussion groups. In Ghana, the instrument is known as "axatse." The gourd has a rounder shape and is usually surrounded with a widely braided net of seeds or nuts. Ghanaian players hang the shékere around the body and beat on the net with their hands. The Brazilian version is known as the "Xeque Bum." The net on this instrument is left open at the bottom.

Of course, in this modern technological age, there is also a fiberglass version of the shékere. The sounding body is made of thin fiberglass layers, and is covered with a network of small glass beads.

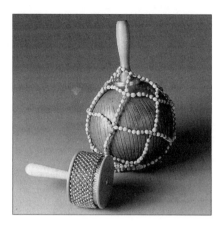

Cabasa

The Brazilian afoche was the inspiration for this modern instrument. The afoche, like the shékere, has a resonating body made of a gourd encased in a network threaded with seeds, but this is a vulnerable construction, and if it is played intensely, the afoche is easily broken. This problem gave rise to a completely new construction that is much stronger than the original, and is known as cabasa. Instead of a gourd, the instrument consists of a plastic or metal sound box, surrounded by a grooved metal plate. The traditional network is replaced by a network of silver-plated steel wires and beads. With the sound box in the palm of your left hand so that your fingers lightly enclose the metal network, you turn the instrument evenly to the left and right, producing a high, rattling sound that is clearly sharper than that of the afoche. The cabasa pictured here is suitable for studio work. It can also be used as a shaker to make soft, rushing sounds, like the sound of a rattlesnake. The cabasa is used in many different musical styles, such as the bossa nova and pop music.

Another type of cabasa was developed to extend its possibilities. This so-called professional cabasa is made completely of synthetic material. The sound box is made of thin fiberglass panels. The evenly indented surface ensures that the closely-fitting network of colorful synthetic beads creates an attractive rustling sound. A sturdy synthetic handle makes it easy to hold.

Ganza

The ganza is a typical rattling instrument made of a cylindrical metal tube filled with metal particles, large seeds, or small pebbles. It is of African origin and is often confused with another rattle called the chocalho, which is of Indian origin. The ganza is found in different sizes and versions, including those with two or more metal tubes of the same size connected together, or the modern versions consisting of a square or hexagonal tube, known respectively as the square ganza or six-sided ganza. The ganza is common in Brazil, particularly in samba music.

The acoustic sound of this shaken tube in a samba orchestra is so penetrating that it beckons listeners from afar, though when it is in the immediate proximity it keeps people at a distance because of its loud rattling noise. You hold the ganza in your left or right hand at shoulder height. By moving it evenly backward and forward and shaking it, you produce a rhythmical movement. When a particular movement is emphasized as the ganza is shaken, the metal balls in the tube are thrown back at a different speed. This effect is known as "retarding," and it produces a sound that is often heard in samba music. It takes time and patience to master this instrument.

Kayamba

This exotic shaking instrument from Kenya consists of a narrow wooden frame surrounded on both sides with a lattice made of thin reeds. This lattice is so tightly woven that the filling, consisting of small seeds, cannot fall out.

The kayamba comes in different sizes and can be played in three ways. The first is the same as for the rainmaker (see page 95). You can turn the kayamba upside down so that the seeds drop down, producing the sound of rain. If the kayamba is used as a rhythmic instrument, there are two possible combinations of movements. One way is to play it like a ganza. You hold the kayamba with both hands at shoulder height. Moving it evenly forward and back while shaking it, you can produce a pattern of sounds with short accents. The other way is to move the instrument from left to right and back, producing a bright, hissing, rattling sound, like a locomotive, when the movement is performed quickly.

Tambourine

Rattling instruments like this tambourine also belong to the group of idio-phones. Tambourines have a definite place in orchestras, bands, and almost every type of pop and rock music. The bright sound and easy playing style characterize the tambourine, which is probably the most popular shaking instrument. It is found in many different shapes and versions. For example, in addition to tambourines made of wood, there are also those made of plastic. The typical way of playing the tambourine is to shake it evenly while holding it in a vertical position.

The special feature of the round tambourine in the illustration is its resonating handle. Holding this handle firmly or loosely with your fingers has an influence on the subtle nuances in the sound of the instrument. In addition, you can create a woodblock sound, accompanied by a soft tinkling, by directly striking the tambourine's resonator with a wooden stick.

Tambarocca

The tambarocca is a contemporary version of the tambourine with many different aspects, both literally and metaphorically. The instrument has a striking hexagonal frame made of synthetic material and is filled with small metal balls. An ingenious system inside controls the movement of the beads in such a way that the tambarocca can be used primarily as a tambourine, secondly as a shaker, and thirdly as a sound effect instrument, like a rainmaker. You hold the tambarocca in one hand, in a vertical position like the tambourine, moved it evenly to and fro. To use it as a shaker, you hold the instrument with both hands in a horizontal position and move it to and fro. To use the hexagonal instrument as a rainmaker, turn it slowly in a circle in a vertical position.

Block Signal Shaker

The block signal shaker is a hand-held percussion instrument, the construction of which is reminiscent of an elongated tambourine. Two metal plates are attached to each end of a wooden handle, forming a frame. Three metal pins are welded on each side between these plates, each serving as the spindle for four metal discs. Both the plates and the discs have rounded edges. This special construction allows the discs to produce a distinct metallic, sometimes intense, rushing sound.

The rattling sound of the irregularly shaped discs is very loud. However, by playing the tin plates with careful movements, rather like a ganza, the block signal shaker is also suitable for pianissimo musical passages. The tinkling of the metal discs is accompanied by the delicate vibrations of the metal plates. If you want to use the instrument as a tambourine, hold it firmly by the handle and swing it to and fro. You can add emphasis to a rhythm pattern by hitting the instrument against your free hand.

Jingle Sticks

Jingle sticks are a special version of the tambourine. The sticks are about one foot long, and six pairs of bells are set within the straight frame. Jingle sticks were originally made to be used as drumsticks. Interesting combinations and sound effects can be produced by using the sticks on instruments such as drums, cymbals, blocks etc. Compared with the classical tambourine, jingle sticks allow for new playing techniques and different sound variations when they are used independently as shaking instruments, precisely because you use both hands, rather than one hand, as with the conventional tambourine. For example, it is easier to play fast rhythmic passages or rolls with jingle sticks; you can produce shaker effects and rolls by moving the two jingle sticks horizontally and vertically.

Triple Castanets

The sound of this curious-looking shaking instrument is somewhat reminiscent of the sound of the Chinese opera. Three narrow plates are attached to a sturdy metal frame in the shape of a loop. A metal pin is welded to each of these plates, and two large metal bells (with a diameter of approximately 10 cm) are attached to these pins so that there are six bells altogether. The bell facing the plates can move freely, while the other bell is welded to the top of the metal pin. When you hold the instrument so that the bells are pointing up, and move it down rapidly at 180°, you'll get a loud, short, jingling noise. When you make the movement in the other direction, the metal plates continue to sound loudly for a long time until they come to rest. You can vary the pattern of sound by shaking the castanets slowly or quickly.

Jingle Bells

The simplicity of these instruments makes the jingling sound they produce all the more remarkable. There are different versions, but they all have one thing in common: they all have large or small chrome-plated sleighbells. These bells, which produce their sound from the small metal ball inside each spherical bell, are firmly attached to synthetic straps. This basic principle is used in all sorts of models. The "sleighbells on a handle," with 25 bells, are very effective. Two straps with bells are stapled onto the four sides of a wooden stick with a round wooden handle. There are six bells on each side, and the twenty-fifth bell is on the end of the stick. There are two different sizes of bells; the small bells produce a higher sound than the large ones. The sound of these jingle bells conjures up images of sleighs in a wintry landscape. They are used to produce sound effects, and are also very suitable as rhythmic instruments. One way of playing the jingle bells is to hold them in the palm of each hand, then throw them up in the air and catch them, one after the other. This creates an interesting rhythmic jingling.

Ankle Bells

Ankle bells were used in classical Indian dance to adorn the ankles of silk-clad dancers. In the Western world, they are used primarily in rhythmic physical therapy and work on consciousness raising, which usually use simple steps that can be acoustically amplified with a pair of ankle bells. Musicians like Aja Addy sometimes wear ankle bells during performances to give his repetitive dance steps an acoustic emphasis. Of course, they are perfect for producing sound effects.

There are many different types of ankle bells. Ankle bells with two or three rows of bells produce a bright and subtle sound. Ankle bells from Pakistan with five to six rows of bells (up to 50 nickel bells per pair) produce a full, dense sound. Finally, there are also colorful cord or rope ankle bells.

Rakatak

The original form of the African rakatak, the "sennpo" from Senegal, consists of a curved wooden stick with decorated rings made from a gourd. The contemporary versions of the single and double rakatak are small percussion instruments with exceptional sound qualities. The rakatak is made from a single piece of jacaranda wood. It consists of a thin wooden handle which ends in a round, hollow sounding body with two symmetrically-placed slits. The tubular sounding body holds one (for the single rakatak) or two (for the double rakatak) plastic pins with small wooden balls on each end, so that the pins can move freely back and forth. When the rakatak is moved suddenly from left to right, the wooden balls strike against the outside of the hollow body, resulting in a wooden clicking sound. Using this movement, you can play all sorts of different rhythms.

Patum

"Patum," the name for a pair of long plastic tubes of different lengths, is onomatopoeic. When you play at least two of these unattractive instruments together, they produce the sound "PA TUM." The original idea comes from the "stamping tubes" of Hawaii. They must be amongst the simplest and oldest instruments for producing a rhythm. They are long tubes made of cane or bamboo, with which the player stamps on the ground to mark the rhythm of a dance. The discovery of this instrument goes back to the time when grains and other seeds were stamped on to make flour. The stamping was done with a particular rhythm to make the work easier, and later it was accompanied by singing. However, these stamping instruments can also be found in Australia, the Fiji Islands, and in South America, where they are usually made of cane or wood.

The modern "stamping tubes" are made of synthetic material and are between two and three feet long. The length of the tubes determines the pitch of the instrument. A black plastic cap at the bottom end of the tube acts as a membrane, and is the secret of the patum's sound; it holds a carefully weighed selection of small pebbles inside the tube, which produces a sound when moved. In order to prevent the pebbles from falling out, a fine sieve is incorporated into the tube, a little way up from the bottom.

You can play the patum in many different ways. For example, you can hold one tube vertically in each hand and then alternate jerking them down with strong movements, without touching the ground. In this way you can hear the collection of pebbles hitting either the plastic membrane or the sieve. This produces a full, hissing sound. By playing different patums at the same time, you can produce a melodic structure. You can also hold the tube horizontally and shake it like a ganza.

Sound Effect Instruments

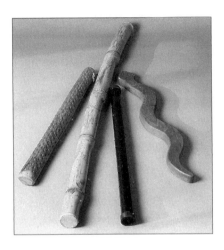

Rainmaker

The precursor of the rainmaker, the guasa, comes from the African and Latin American cultures. The guasa is a shaking tube about three feet long, plaited from fibers, and filled with light seeds. When the tube is turned upside down, the seeds flow down, making a rustling sound. It is used in the music of the Curulao in Columbia.

The modern rainmaker consists of a cylindrical tube, sometimes made of metal, with many pins attached, in a spiral formation, to the inside wall. The small beads inside flow down slowly and evenly when the tube is rotated. The impression of rain falling is imitated perfectly by this ingenious construction of plastic and metal. In the model illustrated here you can even hear a sound like the rushing of the wind: at each end of the tube there is a cap, which has a small hollow space. When you cover the two hollow spaces with your hand and then shake the balls down, you can imitate the sound of the wind by opening and closing the palms of your hands.

Another version of the rainmaker is made of transparent plastic, revealing the way in which the instrument works. Plastic beads gradually filter down to the bottom through plastic discs with holes. The snake rainmaker pictured on the far right, also produces a very delicate sound. It is used predominantly as a shaking instrument, like the ganza. Pictured on the far left is an almost archaic, yet commonly found, type of rainmaker, made from a hollow cactus with sharp thorns on the loose inside, which produce a delicate, warm sound.

Dance Rattle

This rattle is of African origin (Ghana/the Cameroons) and consists of fruit pits, palm seeds, or nuts, which are threaded onto a plaited piece of bark. The flat, oval-shaped dried seeds act simultaneously as a sounding membrane and a resonating body. In order for every seed to achieve its full sound, each one is cracked open in one place without breaking it. When you hold the instrument on one side, the seeds point downward, like grapes on a vine, and produce a rustling sound, especially when you shake them. Originally they were around the waist or legs worn by dancers. The rattles are sometimes called a "crispy," "crispy nuts," or "waterfall." There is a version from Brazil called "goat's nail's," indicating the material used. Imitation fiberglass rattling chains have also been developed in various different sizes, and these are louder than the original instrument.

The effect of this instrument on listeners varies a great deal. The rattle can either beckon, or keep the listener at a distance. When you play it in a penetrating way, it can be very disturbing. Therefore it is important that you consider how it can best be used in a piece of music. This instrument is best for musical pieces with an open beginning or end.

Domino Rattle

You can create all sorts of different rushing sounds with the domino rattle. There are two versions of this instrument: the long kokiriko (originally Japanese), and a shorter, newer version which is approximately 10 inches long. It consists of a broad leather strap, to which 18 wooden plates, each three-eighths of an inch wide, are attached, one next to the other. At each end of the strap, there is a wooden handle, 1-1/2 inches wide. When you hold the handles with both hands so that the domino rattle opens as you bend it, the pieces of wood rub against each other when you move it evenly to and fro.

Cricket

This instrument really does perfectly imitate the song of a cricket on a mild summer's night. Crickets are used in many different forms of disco music, fusion jazz, and pop music.

The construction is simple. Attached to one side of a wooden block is a chromed metal tube with a narrow slit in the middle. In the wood, opposite this slit, there are three holes each of which contains a silver ball. When you slowly tip the cricket down, the three balls come out of their holes, one after the other, and collide against the metal sound box. Because the metal tube is mounted between two pieces of rubber, the resulting sound is a short, dry click, reminiscent of a cricket. You can change the timbre by rotating the metal tube; as you turn the groove further away from the wood block, the sound of the cricket becomes brighter and more open.

Ching Chok

The ching chok has an exotic appearance, as well a unique sound. It is made of a single piece of Asian rosewood. There are two tubular sound boxes of different sizes—each with a resonating slit in the middle—one at each end of a round stick. Two small wooden balls attached to narrow steel springs on each of the sound boxes, strike against the sound boxes when you shake the ching chok evenly backward and forward. The result is a high, percussive sound with two different pitches. When you press the balls on one end against the instrument, so that they can't vibrate, you'll get only one pitch. You can produce a short, vibrating sound by lightly tapping the balls with your finger.

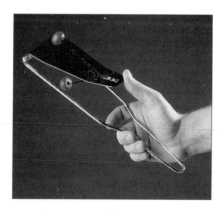

Flex-a-Tone

The name "flex-a-tone" reflects the flexibility of this instrument's tone. The sound of this instrument can be heard on many musical recordings and sound tracks. Although it has a very simple construction, the flex-a-tone produces surprising sound variations. A broad metal plate is attached in a small frame of thick, curved wire. A thin spring with a wooden ball on the end is attached to each side of the metal plate. As you shake the flex-a-tone, the balls strike the plate, which starts to resonate. Pressing and releasing your thumb on the plate while you shake the instrument produces a glissando-like sound effect that can evoke an eerie atmosphere. With a great deal of practice and perseverance, you can produce a simple melody on this percussion instrument (similar to a singing saw). "Theater lightning," a variation on the flex-a-tone, is a long thin steel spring that can be attached at one end to a cymbal stand. By striking the metal spring with a mallet, a short thundering din can be produced.

Vibra-Slap

The vibra-slap is a must for anyone who produces sound effects. Nearly every old horror or gangster film soundtrack features this sound, with its suggestion of chattering teeth and rattling bones, and no studio or theater can manage without it. For this striking effect, musicians in parts of South America still use the old jaw of a donkey (carraca de burro) to accompany their music.

The modern vibra-slap consists of a hollow, wooden resonating body, a metal frame and a sturdy wooden ball. The sound is produced by small metal pins that can move on a metal rail in the resonating body. The vibra-slap is firmly held by a metal frame so that the wooden ball faces upwards. You use the palm of your hand to strike the ball, and the room is filled with chattering, vibrating sounds. You can change or maintain the tone by turning the resonating body. Another variation of the vibra-slap has a round sounding body that extends the rattling sound. This instrument is also different inside:

instead of containing thin metal pins, it has an oval plastic ball attached to a thin spring. This vibra-slap produces a dry, soft tone.

Bar Chimes

As everyone knows from hearing film soundtracks and live music, bar chimes are standard equipment for percussionists these days. The chimes are used when ringing, atmospheric sounds are required. The model illustrated here has 25 gold-colored aluminum bars, suspended from narrow, plastic loops. They give the instrument its rich tone. You play these chimes with the metal stick shown hanging at the end of the wooden bar, to produce eerie, magical sound patterns.

Depending on the nature of their construction and the intervals at which the single metal rods are tuned, each set of bar chimes produces very different patterns of sound. For example, in addition to the standard model, there are modal chimes with a pentatonic scale, or whisper chimes, which are made of extremely thin brass rods that produce a very high, soft, rustling sound. The small round model illustrated in the photograph is a very different version with a unique sound. When you hold all the rods in one hand for a brief moment, and then quickly release them, you get a combination of tones that resound until they slowly come to rest in harmonious tranquillity.

Bell Tree

In Japan, the bell tree is traditionally known as "orugoru," and it is also played in traditional music of Pakistan. You can produce interesting sound effects with the modern version of the bell tree or bar bells. The 14 brass bells are placed close together on an iron rod, mounted in such a way that you can strike them one at a time with a metal mallet, producing a clear tone, or play them all together by running the mallet along the outside of the bells. With this glissando technique, you can produce a spooky sound pattern with a crystal-clear sound that is familiar from the music of old horror films. The instrument can be free-standing, as well as held by its convenient handle. You can achieve a special, magical effect by swinging the bell tree round after striking the bells.

European Bird Calls

A set consists of 28 bird calls, from the blackbird to the blue tit, the nightingale to the wren; all the sounds of European songbirds are represented. A bird lover in France had the idea for this instrument; his aim was to imitate the original quality of each bird as accurately as possible. The collection of sound effects produces clear, differentiated sounds, and is a delight for any percussionist interested in evoking particular moods and effects.

The instruments are made of different materials such as wood, metal and rubber, and are individually wrapped in a wooden case, which contains instructions on how to imitate the bird calls. The results are wonderful: there is a range of cooing, chirruping, cawing and trilling sounds which are often similar to the consonants in human speech. It is no coincidence that many theories about the origin of music are based on birdsong. Without a doubt, there are many elements birdsong that correspond to human singing, particularly among primitive peoples. These instruments are also collected by the hunters.

It is well known that there are all sorts of exotic birds in the Brazilian rainforest. However, few people know that there is a company in Espirito Santo which has specialized in the manufacture of bird pipes since 1903. These pipes were originally used for hunting birds, until musicians of all schools became interested in them. There are 33 beautifully made pipes in all, and they come in an equally exquisite wooden case. Each of the pipes is made of rosewood, and accurately imitates the sound of a Brazilian bird. For example, the bird call, "Capueiro ou Uru," the largest pipe in the set, produces the sound by means of a small pipe of synthetic material flying round in a resonating space, which is the same principle used for a referee's whistle. By pressing down on the air hole in the sound box, you can produce a deeper tone. Alternating the high and deep notes produces the bird song of the Capueiro ou Uru. The jac, or zabelé birdcall, is made by another sort of pipe, also known as a nose flute. It is made of steel or wood. You place the sound box of the flute against your nose, and you lightly press the soft metal part against your lower lip. You produce melodies by exhaling softly through your nose into the visible opening, while changing the shape of your mouth.

Apito

The apito is a Brazilian whistle and is used for signaling, as well as for indicating rhythm. In the samba batucada, the apito is used to signal agreed-upon breaks (interruptions) to the other players. For example, there are apito patterns which open or end a batucada. The original samba whistle is made of Brazilian hardwood. It is one of a large group of whistles from Brazil. The apito can produce three tones if the small holes on the side are opened or closed with the fingers to change the pitch. This small percussion instrument is known in the trade as the tri-tone whistle and can also be made of metal or plastic, as well as wood. Metal has the advantage that of producing a louder, more shrill tone, so that the signals in a large batucada can be heard very clearly. A wooden apito sounds warmer, and more like a bird call.

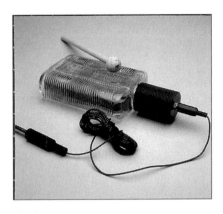

Singing Bottle

Everyone has heard the glugging sound that is produced when a half-empty wine bottle is moved gently back and forth. This sound effect is imitated by the singing bottle. The bottle, which is about 7 inches tall, is filled with water up to 5/6 of its height. A flat amplifier is stuck onto the outside of the bottle. Plugs and electronic parts are concealed in the top of the bottle. The striking thing about the singing bottle is the large variety of possible sound effects. For example, there is the broad range of bubbling sounds that are created by holding the bottle in your hand and moving it so that the liquid inside slaps against the wall of the bottle. In addition, you can use a metal mallet with a cork head, to strike the side of the bottle, for a percussive effect. At the same time, you can modulate the pitch by turning the bottle. Lastly, you can also produce a guiro effect, if you run the handle of the mallet over the ribs of the bottle. Again, the pitch can be varied. The singing bottle is eminently suitable for experimenting with sound effects.

Gongs and Sound Plates

Gongs

In the Malay language, percussion instruments are generally called "gongs." In principle, musicologists call all bronze instruments consisting of a circular plate with a curved edge from which it is suspended, gongs. The gong serves as a symbol to remind us of our common origin. There are gongs with a dome in the middle, like the Burma gong or the Javanese bonang. Gongs with a flat playing surface and a curved edge are also known as a tam-tam.

All gongs produce a basic tone with a harmonic spectrum that varies in scope, depending on the structure of the instrument. The gong's timbre can be influenced in many ways, including the way in which the gong is struck and the beater that is used.

The sound of a gong is produced by the experienced hands of a gong builder, who uses his intuition, as well as technical criteria, to work the metal. The instruments imported from Eastern Asia are made in four stages: they are cast, forged, retouched, and tuned. When they are cast, copper and tin are melted to produce a flat bronze disc, or "lakar". The gong is constantly rotated while it is glowing red hot, and hammered until the right shape is achieved. For retouching and tuning the gong, the material is polished, and when the metal has cooled down, it is hammered again. The dome in the middle of some gongs is essential for the quality of their sound. The dome determines the tone and prevents harmonic vibrations from spreading from one side to the other, thereby reinforcing the volume of the basic tone.

Burma Gong

Burma gongs have a dome in the center, and when this is struck, the most beautiful sound is produced: a linear, concentrated, and transparent sound. These gongs are made in sizes from 8 to 25 inches. When several Burma gongs are played together, the meditative, soothing waves continue for a long time. There is good reason why the gong symbolizes the principle of timelessness, the return to silence, and the removal of a concept of space and time. Large Burma gongs produce an extremely warm, powerful sound with a deep bass tone.

Tuned Gongs

Like the Burma gong, tuned gongs have a dome in the center, but the gong-smith has used his expertise to tune them to a precise pitch. This type of gong originates from Southeast Asia: Bali, Java, Thailand and Burma. Nowadays, tuned gongs, like symphonic gongs (see below), are made of a thin bronze plate and the pitch is electronically checked so that it is possible to play it with other tuned instruments.

Tuned gongs are available with different tones and in every desired combination from C2/C to F6/f''', together with the appropriate stands and drumsticks. Because of their particularly warm, clear timbre, tuned gongs are an interesting addition to many ensembles.

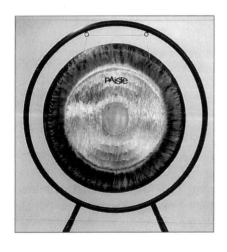

Symphonic Gong

The symphonic gong is an untuned flat gong with a slightly concave membrane. The instrument pictured here is made in Germany. In contrast with the traditional gongs, which are cast our of a metal plate, the symphonic gong is made from a cold-rolled bronze plate. This construction allows the metal disc to vibrate more freely, and the harmonics are reflected more often in the sounding surface. The characteristics of these flat gongs are the dynamics of the sound as a whole: from the rushing, sparkling, high tones to the clearly identifiable bass tone. Symphonic gongs are available in diameters from 20 inches to 6-1/2 feet. The pressure of the sound waves can be felt physically from a distance of three feet. This is a very suitable instrument for sound therapy.

Planet Gong

The characteristic sound of the planet gong is comparable to that of the symphonic gongs ranging between a diameter of 20 inches to 3 feet. Because of the special way in which they are tuned, they have represented the music of the spheres since classical times. The concept of cosmic harmony is a theme that has captured the human imagination in almost every culture: it is one of the archetypal concepts in Western and Eastern civilization.

The sound produced by planet gongs is powerful and mysterious, with a clear bass tone (untempered tuning), tuned to the natural series of harmonics of the Earth, the Moon, the Sun and the planets. They are designed to vibrate in harmony with the orbits of celestial bodies. The basic calculations for this type of sound instrument were made by Hans Cousto, who wrote *The Cosmic Octave*.[14]

Sound Creation Gong

Sound creation gongs are made using the same process as the symphonic gong and were developed in the search for differentiated sounds. With the

---

[14] Hans Cousto, *The Cosmic Octave* (Mendocino: LifeRhythm, 1988).

help of surveys, corresponding impressions of sound characteristics were determined which led to the perfection of this set of gongs.

Making a gong requires a great deal of know-how. The most difficult thing is to tune the gong so that the desired sound characteristic is achieved; sometimes several attempts have to be made. This is certainly the case for the sound creation gong. Every one of these gongs is completely different in appearance and timbre. These differences result in an impressive range of sounds, evoking the most diverse perceptions. The large range of timbres leads to extremely individual ways of playing them to produce interesting combinations and applications of sound. Sound creation gongs are symbolically associated with the four elements of earth, water, fire, and air. For example, there is a moon gong and a fire gong (see illustration).

Chinese Opera Gongs

These two types of gong come from the orchestras of the Chinese opera (the Peking Opera). Their most characteristic quality is a short glissando-like change in pitch immediately after they have been struck. At first, this sound has a very curious and sometimes frightening effect on the listener.

The largest type of opera gong, the "fu-in-luo," has an elusive bass tone that quickly dies away. With a "normal" gong, this effect would only be possible if the instrument were submerged in water immediately after being struck. The fu-in-luo gongs are available in three sizes.

The glissando effect of the other, smaller type of opera gong works conversely to that of the fu-in-luo: the high bass tone floats up, accompanied by a light crash. Two gongs of the same size (about 8 inches) can produce two different pitches. In all opera gongs, the glissando effect becomes stronger if you strike them with greater force, and you strike the beater against the raised, thin-walled center of the instrument. These gongs are ideal wherever unusual sounds are needed.

Feng Luo

The feng luo is a cymbal gong. This gold-colored sounding instrument is made of a brass disc about 1/16 of an inch thick, with clearly visible grooves on both sides. Small indentations are made in these with a hammer in the traditional way for Chinese gongs.

If you hold the gong horizontally at eye level, you will see that its outer edge is slightly curved inward. The feng luo can easily be suspended from a stand by a fray-resistant cord threaded through the two holes in the disc. In order to play the feng luo, you need a soft, fabric-covered beater.

The fascinating aspect of this Chinese percussion instrument is the broad spectrum of sounds that can be produced when you strike the metal disc with varying intensity. The sound ranges from warm, rounded tones at the deep end of the spectrum, up to a silvery rustling sound at very high frequencies.

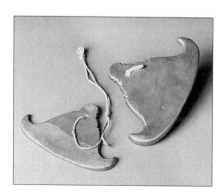

Kung Zee

This Burmese temple bell has an almost triangular, flat metal sounding body, and is freely suspended by a cord through the top corner. It is made in many different sizes, and is characterized by a long drawn-out, singing bell-like sound. You beat it with a small mallet. For a rounded, singing vibrato effect, you can strike one of the two bottom corners of the kung zee (or kyeeze) so that the instrument quickly starts to rotate.

Related to the kyeeze are the Indian krotales and Tibetan tingshas; these are two thick metal cymbals, joined together with a strap through the center. When you strike them against each other, so that the edges touch, they produce a very clear, penetrating sound.

Sound Plates and Sound Discs

The sound plate's music is reminiscent of the ringing of bells, a sound of great beauty. A sound plate is a rectangular bronze plate with a slightly rough surface. When suspended from a spring, the sound plate can vibrate freely, producing a long-lasting sound. You can produce very different harmonics and timbres, which are a delight to the ear, when you play it with a small mallet or with wooden sticks. Sound plates come in four different sizes (18' x 12', 13' x 9', 12' x 8', and 10' x 7'), which are all tuned to their own sound level, as well as to each other.

The sound disc is a flat, round bronze alloy disc, which is suspended from a cord. When you strike it with a small mallet, the disc produces an unusually clear and brilliant, long-resounding tone. You can also pass the bow of a double bass along the edge of the instrument, while holding it by the cord with your other hand; this results in extremely high harmonics. If you then make the sound disc swing to and fro, a floating vibrato effect is produced. Sound discs can be played separately or in any combination. They come in different sizes, and are the modern version of the Burma temple bell.

Other Instruments

Singing Bowls

The floating sound of these round metal bowls, which mainly originate from Nepal, has a direct effect on our feelings. There are all sorts of different theories about their origin and use. Traditionally, the bowls were made by hand from an alloy of seven metals—gold, silver, mercury, copper, iron, tin and lead—each of which relates to a planet. Each metal has its own frequency, and the different frequencies combine to create the richly harmonic singing sound. The proportion of the different metals used to make a singing bowl determines its sound as well as its appearance. The size of the bowl, and the thickness of the metal also affects the bowl's timbre. Singing bowls come in all sorts of shapes and sizes.

Singing bowls are played by striking them with a beater, or the edge can be rubbed with a smooth wooden stick, which produces a singing tone that sounds for a long time. To do this, place the bowl on the palm of your hand, on a slightly springy base, or on a hard cushion. In addition to the well-known singing bowls from Tibet (matte-colored because of a high silver and tin content), Nepal (shiny, golden color), and Indian bowls, there are also Chinese and Japanese bowls, which are made of different alloys. The Japanese temple bell, the "dobachi," is a large, black metal bowl that is usually placed on a silk cushion on a special wooden stand. It is struck with a leather-covered wooden stick, producing a dry, bright sound.

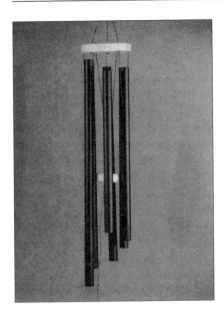

Wind Chimes

The principle of wind chimes is very simple: a number of tubes of unequal length are suspended from a circular plate by a cord or strap, so that they can move freely. In the middle, a small disc or ball made of hard material is also suspended by a cord to serve as a clapper. When it strikes the tubes, they sound. Hanging below the clapper, on the same cord, there is a flat wind catcher which hangs down below the tubes. The wind chimes are placed inside or outside in a draft, and the wind does the rest: it blows unevenly, so that the clapper starts to move and the tubes begin to sound in an arbitrary order. Wind chimes are made in all sorts of materials: bamboo, glass, as well as the metal chimes illustrated here. These wind chimes, with a total length of four feet, are not only the largest of their sort, but also the loudest. The sound produced by these black anodized aluminum tubes, 1-1/2 inches thick, is a deep bass tone. The six tubes vibrate at intervals of a C sharp pentatonic scale. Moved by hand or by the wind, a multitude of bell-like melodies can be produced. With the chimes pictured here, the sound is produced by a wooden disc in the middle, and a thick piece of wood serves as the wind catcher. Any music lover will be transported by the soothing metallic sounds. In addition to wind chimes made with tubes as sounding bodies, there are also wind chimes with fired clay discs, and others made of shells (shell wind chimes).

Kalimba

This instrument, also known as the African thumb piano, sansas, or mbira, is a plucked instrument. It consists of a sound box with a hole cut into the lid. A number of strips of springy steel are attached to this lid in such a way that the end of the strips can vibrate freely above the hole. The pitch of a strip is determined by its length. The instrument is very easy to tune because of the way in which the strips are attached to the instrument. The metal strips are placed on two bridges running across the instrument. A metal rail presses down on the strips between these bridges. The rail can be secured onto the lid with two screws, and it can also be loosened, so that the strips can easily be adjusted.

To play the kalimba, hold it in both hands with your fingers under the sound box and pluck the strips with both thumbs. Sometimes there are two more holes in the bottom of the sound box which you can cover with your fingers to change the sound. The kalimbas illustrated here produce a playful sound, reminiscent of music boxes. Kalimbas with a mahogany lid and a gourd as a sound box have a the warmer, deeper timbre. Sometimes the bottom of the gourd is beautifully decorated. A kalimba made entirely of wood is richer in harmonics.

Marimbula

This curious instrument is a larger version of the kalimba. The marimbula is the original bass played in the Caribbean. The sound box is pine, and measures approximately 16' x 24'. It has a cover with two resonating holes. The eight large chrome-plated steel springs, each half an inch wide, are particularly striking. You can tune them by unscrewing three wing nuts so that there is some give in the hardwood plate which presses the springs firmly onto two strips of wood, and you can move the springs slightly. Played together, the springs produce a beautiful sound. You can play the marimbula either with your fingers or with mallets. When you strike it with a mallet, the springs resonate with fresh overtones. This instrument can also be classified as a percussion instrument.

To play the marimbula while standing up, you need a guitar strap with screws to attach it to the instrument. It then hangs in front of your stomach so that you can easily play it with your fingers.

Mouth Harp

The mouth harp is one of the plucked idiophones. It is a natural instrument with an enchanting sound, depending upon how you shape your oral cavity while playing it. The instrument consists of a bamboo or metal frame containing a sounding spring. You hold the instrument between your lips and pluck the spring with a finger. Your oral cavity—the inside of your mouth, and even your throat—acts as a resonating chamber. If the shape of your mouth and throat constantly change (soundlessly forming vowels), as in harmonic singing, the mouth harp will also produce harmonics in different pitches. By breathing in and out rhythmically, you can produce some really folksy sounds.

The most commonly found mouth harps are made of metal and the frame is in the shape of a loop containing a steel spring to produce the sound. The mouth harps illustrated in the photographs are Philippine mouth harps, made of narrow bamboo strips, from which the sounding tongues have been cut. These mouth harps are about seven inches long and are delicately decorated on the surface with animal-like figures. It is a small miracle that such a harmonious percussion instrument can be made from a flat piece of bamboo!

Gopichand

This strange-looking percussion instrument from India is a Bengali plucked drum, often used by street musicians. People who live on the streets in India, without a possession in the world, try to earn a few rupees by playing the gopichand. The instrument looks like a small drum with protuberances, but it is plucked rather than beaten. The gopichand has a fine metal wire in the middle, which is connected on one end to the goat skin stretched across the small wooden sound box, and at the other end to the knob on a long wooden bracket. To ensure that the wire does not damage the skin, it is first attached to a thin metal plate to prevent tearing. The string can be tuned to the desired pitch with a screw that acts rather like the tuning keys of a violin; this reveals the special quality of the instrument. When you first pluck it, the sounds do not seem particularly interesting, but when you squeeze the flexible wooden bracket at the same time, some fascinating variations happen. Glissando-like changes in pitch give the delicate sound a melancholic quality, yet this Bengali plucking drum is also perfect for accompanying musical performances in which humor plays a role.

Berimbão

In jazz, pop and folk music, percussion instruments of many different kinds are used, including the berimbão, the Brazilian musical bow with a gourd resonator. It was originally from Angola, and is the instrument of the capoeira, a sport which combines martial arts and dancing. The berimbão is an elegant instrument that produces a penetrating bass tone. It has a simple construction. A steel string, or *corda,* is stretched on a stick made of biriba wood. A resonator—a half-open gourd, or *cabaca,* is tied firmly, with a piece of string, around the stick and wire. You hold the stick in one hand vertically in front of your body. When you play the berimbão, you open and close the gourd by pressing the open half against your stomach, and moving it away again, with a movement of the stick, to produce the characteristic wah-wah sound. The wire is struck with a thin wooden stick, or *vaqueta.* The hand with which you use the *vaqueta* also holds a caxixi, which accompanies the sound of the berimbão. A very proficient player can shorten the steel string with a coin or a flat stone held between the thumb and the index finger of the hand that holds the bow, so that a second tone can be heard as well as the bass tone, which approximates the interval of a major second. After playing the berimbão, the steel string should be loosened, so that the bow retains its flexibility.

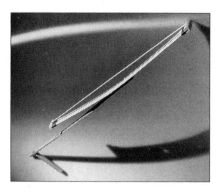

Humming Bow

The sound of this instrument takes the listener back about 25,000 years. The Aborigines of New Zealand and Australia still use the traditional nose bow today in their rituals. It is attached to a string by which it is swung round, vibrating the air to produce a humming sound. The humming bow is a new creation, based on this ancient principle. For a humming bow, a special thin strip of synthetic material is stretched across a piece of bamboo of varying length and width. The bamboo is slightly bent by the tightness of the synthetic "string." This sounding body is attached with two tacks to a thin wooden strip. At the end of this strip of wood, there is a moveable wooden handle. You hold the humming bow by the handle and swing it around, so that the synthetic string vibrates. This produces an enchanting humming bass tone, which transports us into the world of spirits and our ancestors. By changing the speed of rotation, you can change the pitch of the tones. This is an extremely dynamic instrument to play.

Bull Roarer

You can buy this ribbed plastic tube (about three feet long) in most well-stocked toy shops. It looks rather like a brightly colored vacuum cleaner hose, but it's called a bull roarer.

It is extremely easy to play. You hold one end of the tube firmly, and swing it around above your head. It produces a curious, floating, singing sound. Higher and lower tones can be produced by changing the speed at which you swing it. The distance between the various tones corresponds to the structure of a series of harmonics. If you hold the tube a little way from the end, or cut off a piece, the air column is shortened, resulting in a different bass tone; in this way, you can experiment with two tubes of different lengths.

Didgeridoo

There is an ancient legend, which is still told today, about the original inhab-
itants of Australia, the Aborigines: thousands of years ago, a woman went
out to gather wood. She didn't notice that one of the trunks was hollow. Suddenly, the wind started to blow. It blew all day long, and while it blew, a
strange unknown sound could be clearly heard. The members of the tribe
looked for the origin of the sound and discovered the hollow tree trunk.
They said, "If the wind can produce such a sound from a hollow tree trunk,
why shouldn't we?" Since those days, the didgeridoo has been played by
men. Its name is the English version of the aboriginal word.

How is a didgeridoo made? It's very simple: the Aborigines look for
eucalyptus trees hollowed out by termites, and then saw off the hollow
branches, which are between one and four inches in diameter. These can
then be used to make didgeridoos. A beeswax mouthpiece is added to make
the instrument easier to blow into.

You make the didgeridoo sound by blowing into it with completely
relaxed lips. It's easy to make the mistake of blowing into it as if you were
playing a horn, with compressed cheeks or pursed lips. The vibration of the
lips produces an enchanting bass tone. The important thing is not to create
melodies with natural tones, as in the case with classical wind instruments,
but to develop a single tone. The difficult technique of circular breathing
(simultaneously breathing in through the nose and out through the mouth)
enables the musician to have seemingly limitless breath, so that he can sus-
tain a single note for several minutes. It is with the complete control of this
technique that the characteristic, enchanting sound of the instrument can be
achieved. By means of a special technique with the larynx and oral cavity,
and by changing the pattern of breathing, the player can imitate the sound of
dingoes, kangaroos, the rolling of thunder and the rushing of the wind, as

well as all sorts of bird calls. The didgeridoo is often accompanied by the rhythmic clapping of sticks (clap sticks).

Anklung

This percussion instrument from Southeast Asia is a standard instrument for folk music in Indonesia, Thailand and Laos. At first sight, it's hard to tell what you're supposed to do with it, but once you pick up the instrument and discover its sound, it becomes fascinating.

The anklung is a bamboo rattle, and therefore it should really be included in the group of shaking instruments, but its melodic sound defies classification. The instrument produces such a range of different, delicate, warm, clear wooden sounds that in Indonesia there are whole anklung orchestras that play melodies. The instrument consists of at least three bamboo pipes which are tuned in octaves; the size of the pipe determines the pitch. The vertical pipes are suspended on a horizontal bamboo pole in such a way that they can be easily moved back and forth. The construction results in click-clacking sounds of different speeds and pitches. This bamboo rattle can be used as a sound effect instrument or can provide a rhythm. With a bit of imagination, you can develop your own music on this instrument.

Waterphone

This instrument was developed by Dick Waters from California. Nevertheless, the instrument mainly owes its name to the fact that it uses water. The waterphone is played with a violin bow, and consists of a flat container in which several thin brass rods of different lengths are welded. A hollow tube ending in a funnel rises up from the center of the container.

To play the waterphone, you first pour a glass of water into the container through the funnel. Then you hold the instrument by the funnel in one hand, in such a way that the brass tubes, which each have their own pitch, can be vibrated by playing them with a rosined bow. In addition to the bass tones, you can hear numerous harmonics that resonate in the sound box. When you move the water in the container slightly by gently rocking the instrument, these delicate harmonic vibrations combine to produce subtle atmospheric sounds which resonate for a long time. The sounds produced by a waterphone are comparable to flageolet tones played on a muted violin string or produced by rubbing the finger around the wet rim of a wine glass.

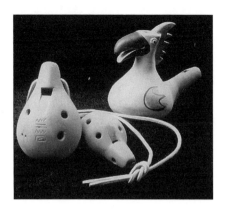

Ocarina

These fired clay whistles are found in all sorts of different versions and pitches, such as soprano, sopranino and alto. Every instrument has six openings which can be covered with the thumb, index finger and middle finger of each hand. When the sound opening is shut, this produces a pleasant, deep bass tone. When it is open, a bright, clear tone can be heard. By covering different openings, you can produce more than eight tones.

There are different kinds of animal-shaped ocarinas. For example, the small earthenware tortoise shown here can be worn around the neck on a leather thong. The bird-shaped whistles are the most popular for their warbling sound, which is created by filling the whistle, through the beak, with water, and blowing into the tail end. There are four models of the bird whistles, but the differences are more in the original, imaginative, and sometimes comical shapes, than in the sound that is produced.

Triple-tone Whistle

The simple construction of this instrument is all the more surprising when you blow the black plastic mouthpiece for the first time. The three chrome-plated iron tubes are precisely tuned to a D triad, and produce a sound that unmistakably reproduces the sound of a train or tug whistle. Two notes can be played together by opening or shutting the individual tubes. The small hook on the middle tube makes it possible to hang the instrument on a belt. The whistle comes in two sizes: 6 inches (small triple-tone whistle) and 12 inches, and there is also a version with four tones. The pitch is different in each of these whistles, but the train effect remains the same. The smallest whistle is easiest to use musically. You can see players of the hand drum in the samba batucada holding this instrument with their teeth. The higher pitch of the small whistle comes into its own among the sounds of a large bateria de samba, or a big band.

Part 4

Rhythm Basics

Elementary Experience of Rhythm

The Basic Pulse

Among one of the greatest mysteries of life is what has been described by musicologists as the "soundless pulse of rhythm." What is this soundless pulse? Is it a source of energy? A formula? Perhaps, even, the secret of life? Is it the phenomenon that drives thinkers, artists, and scientists, in their attempts at universal understanding?

No one has yet been able to provide a perfect description of the perfect rhythm. But the attempt to achieve it can act as an inspiration, and help you think about the natural pulse and rhythm of your own life. Perhaps this explains the enthusiasm for African and other forms of rhythmical music which can increasingly be heard in the Western world. The theme of rhythm, which is not only an elementary building block in music, but also permeates many areas of our society, is as fascinating as it is varied. Our whole existence is subject to rhythms and cycles that affect us: day and night, weeks and their recurrent division into seven days, and the annual movement of the Earth around the Sun. In the natural world there is the cycle of the seasons from Spring to Summer, Autumn and Winter, which consciously or unconsciously influences our feelings. In our own breathing we hear the triple rhythm of breathing in, breathing out, and pausing, and our heart has a two-stroke rhythm of systole and diastole.

In fact, all rhythms can be reduced to the numbers 2 and 3. Assuming that the mother's heartbeat is our first experience of rhythm, it becomes clear why we are unable to escape the influence of rhythm, and why the heartbeat forms the primitive pulse of music in every culture. In his book, *The Forgotten Power of Rhythm*, Reinhard Flatischler describes the interrelationship between pulsation and the body:

"The heartbeat is a complicated rhythmic event; but we can experience it as a simple, supportive pulsation anywhere within the body where the pulse can be felt. We *hear* music with our body and *play* music with our body. The body and its rhythms play a central role in music. This is why we find a knowledge of the inner pulse in the music of all cultures. There are drums which directly imitate the melody of the heartbeat. The drumming of Native American shamans involves a direct musical transposition of the heartbeat, and, so, too, do certain rhythms played on the Korean *buk* and the Japanese *taiko*. The heartbeat also forms the rhythmic foundation for complex Indian rhythms." [15]

Rhythm and Power

When I hear Brazilian or African music, I am always inspired by the power of this drum music and its enduring influence on my whole person. Something in me starts to move with the music. I feel the quiet and the strong accents that give the rhythm its vibrating tension. Since I have become interested in the percussion music of other cultures, my impression has been confirmed that people who experience these vibrations, as well as people who do rhythmical, physical work, can change their lives in a positive way.

The inner power of rhythm can be experienced not only in music, but also in daily life. Everyone knows the feeling of relaxation experienced when you walk through woods or fields, or the feeling of being on the same wavelength when you are talking to other people, or walking on a sidewalk along with a crowd of people who are all stepping in rhythm. At these moments, we feel at one with everything, free of doubt, and with a sense of being uplifted. Seeing a successful pirouette by a figure skater can produce this feeling. Thus it is not surprising that many cultures, such as the African, Japanese, Indian, Chinese and Indonesian cultures, are familiar with the concept of a source of power that permeates everything in existence.

The search for the ultimate source of all the forces that fundamentally connect the life of people, animals, plants and the universe, has given rise to a modern view of the universe as being engaged in a perpetual cosmic dance. Scientific discoveries have long indicated that we are subject to rhythms at every level, whether at an atomic, organic or social level, and that there is a single common law, a common order. When we reject this cosmic order, it inevitably creates a crisis at every level of human existence. In a society which has developed as far as ours, dividing time into hours, minutes, seconds and nanoseconds—which prevents us from finding our own rhythm because it is so strictly regulated—it's not surprising that depression is a common problem, and that people try to escape from this artificial rhythm.

---

[15]   Reinhard Flatischler, *The Forgotten Power of Rhythm*, (Mendocino: LifeRhythm, 1992) p. 93.

We all carry the order of the world within us, and resonate with the rhythm of the cosmos. When you make arrangements with a friend to meet for dinner and a movie, it's like a dance carried out with great precision. Even casual conversation has the purpose of producing a resonance between two or more people.

Rhythm is a universal language and an expression of the soul. It is part of everyday life, lives in our hearts, and reveals itself when we interrupt our daily routine. Many of us live with our heads, on the basis of rationality and logic, alienated from the true source of personal strength, creativity. Creativity means making new forms out of making choices. It allows for the possibility of freeing the self of habits and rigid lifestyles. Where creativity is suppressed, violence and insensitivity take over. If we see creativity as leading us towards our natural impulses, as encouraging us to liberate the body and playfully stimulating us to free the psyche, we will discover a strength in ourselves that allows for a process of consciousness and purification. All of this involves placing our thoughts, actions, and desires in an ethical context which I would describe with the words: reason, respect and responsibility.

It's easy to notice when we are no longer in the rhythm or current of life. It makes us feel unwell and cut off from the basic movements of life. Just as a small child needs a mother's heartbeat to develop in a world without time and space, humanity needs the pulse of the world as a whole, the memory of the archetypal patterns which allow life to go on and which form the basic rhythm of our existence. With music, rhythm and sound, we have a vehicle with which we can experience the laws of life, as well as those of music.

Learning Basic Rhythms

In this chapter, I invite you to learn the musical movement of the numbers two and three. Two and three can be multiplied by themselves to produce four, six and nine-beat rhythms, and can also be combined to produce five and seven-beat rhythms. The sequence of syllables KA LE BA SHI represents the four-beat units, while U ME LA represent the three-beat units. This pattern of syllables was developed by Rolf Exler, and serves to familiarize beginners with the pattern of the four- and three-beat pulse, from which countless rhythms and musical styles have been derived. Musical styles based on a four-beat pulse are described as binary (consisting of two parts) rhythms, such as funk, rock, marching music, and pop. Musical styles that swing in with a three-beat pulse are described as ternary rhythms and include the shuffle, swing music, and boogie-woogie. There are styles in which binary and ternary rhythms are combined, such as in samba music, or Cuban and Puerto Rican music. The binary basic rhythm (a four-beat pulse) is combined with ternary elements (three-beat pulse).

The basic rhythm exercises I present here are based primarily on the above-mentioned patterns of syllables. They are aimed at allowing you to experience the rhythmic expression of three and four beats. It is much easier to intensely experience the feeling of a flowing pulse by pronouncing the syllables in sequence, rather than by counting numbers out loud.

The method is as follows: the pulse and structure of the basic rhythm exercises can easily be followed and experienced with the help of simple dance steps, spoken syllables, and by clapping the hands. You can then use these basic rhythms on many different percussion instruments, whether they come from Africa, Latin America or Asia.

However, before discussing the exercises, I would like to start by raising the following question: how do African drummers manage to make their rhythms flow so irresistibly, and express them in such differentiated ways that these vibrations are directly transferred to us? A clear sense of the pulse and control of beat and off-beat form the basis of their rhythmic actions. African music is off-beat music. You could also say that the beat of a rhythm contains a large number of accents. It is absolutely essential to achieve a rhythmic base and incorporate the beat and off-beat into your own system.

A flowing, rhythmic movement starts with your own pulse and respiratory cycle. This is the starting point for experiencing the body's rhythm. You start by becoming aware of your own pulse. In your body, it is clear that the contraction and relaxation of the heart muscle are equally important activities, and that the one cannot exist without the other. The diastole, together with the systole, forms the rhythmic, alternating contraction and relaxation of the heart. When this is transferred to music, it results in the direct experience of the pulse and the alternate stressed and unstressed beats (see Table 1.1).

By seeing the body as an instrument, we are able to understand the possible rhythms and experience them in their totality. With the voice, feet and hands, we have three levels of rhythmic expression: the voice participates to give the pulse, while the feet carry the beat. Clapping the hands determines the form and introduces accents. In contrast with counting one, two, three and so on, it is easier to experience a flowing pulse by using syllables. Before learning the four-beat rhythm in the next chapter, it is important to start by speaking or singing the syllables evenly.

1. Four-Beat Pulse

The patterns in Tables 1.1 to 6.1, should help you thoroughly master the exercises that follow them. The large dots indicate where the major accents should be placed. Pattern a shows that the smallest common rhythmic denominator is the pulse. It is subdivided into heavy and light accents. The beating heart is a simple example for these accents. You could say: contraction = beat, relaxation = off-beat.

Before starting on the exercises, I would like to explain the four-step, the basis of many ethnic dances. What is the energetic or philosophical principle of the four-step? In the four-step, the right and left halves of the body are combined in a single flowing movement by means of two steps with the right foot and two with the left. In terms of energy, the right and left sides symbolize the polarity principle of yin and yang, to which Chinese philosophy ascribes a number of different characteristics. The right represents the male principle, the active element, giving, and the daytime. The left represents, among other things, the female principle, the passive element, receiving, and the night. This classification does not entail any value judgments, but merely serves to explain that in a balanced co-operation of the two elements of energy, there is a meaningful whole. When this principle is applied to the four-step, it gives you the opportunity to experience your self and your body as a whole in the total process of the movements. In this way you can experience your own focus. A small tip: start by concentrating entirely on the successive steps for a while, without singing the syllables. Create a small dance with this four-step and see what happens to you.

All the exercises are developed on the basis of this four-step. The starting position is standing with your feet parallel to each other, about the width of a foot apart. In this way, you form an inner contact with the ground.

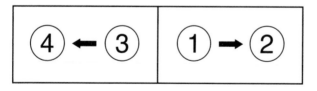

Four-Step

First step: raise your right foot and place it down (again) next to your left foot (1).

Second step: place your right foot out to the side about two foot widths from your left foot (2).

Third step: place your left foot parallel next to your right foot (3).

Fourth step: place your left foot out to the side about two foot widths from your right foot (4). Then place the right foot next to the left foot again (1).

In this way your body moves rhythmically from left to right and back again. Every time your right foot is placed next to your left foot, the cycle starts again from the beginning. After a while, you can sing the syllables KA LE BA SHI to accompany every step. By repeating the sequences of KA LE BA SHI four times, you create a regular pulse with four beats (steps).

Table 1.1: Pulse

·	·	·	·	·	·	·	·	·	·	·	·	·	·	·	·	Pulse
●	·	●	·	●	·	●	·	●	·	●	·	●	·	●	·	Contraction
·	●	·	●	·	●	·	●	·	●	·	●	·	●	·	●	Relaxation

Table 1.2: Beat and Off-beat

	KA	LE	BA	SHI	KA	LE	BA	SHI	KA	LE	BA	SHI	KA	LE	BA	SHI	Pulse/Voice
Fig. 1	●				●				●				●				Feet
Fig. 2			●				●				●				●		Hands
Fig. 3		●		●		●		●		●		●		●		●	Hands

Beat and Off-beat

With the help of Table 1.2, you can experience the rhythm simply with the accent on the first beat (fig. 1), the off-beat (fig. 2), and the double off-beat (fig. 3). The perfect mastery of the off-beat is a precondition for any rhythmic action. You start with a basis—the four-step—and after you're comfortable with this, say the syllables KA LE BA SHI accompanying every step. If you then emphasize the flowing pulse on the syllable BA, first only with the voice, and then by clapping your hands, you will hear the simple off-beat, a rhythmic stylistic element in, for example, reggae music. Emphasizing the syllables LE and SHI enables you to feel and hear the double off-beat. This rhythmical element can be found in samba and funk music.

Here is another exercise: go back to the basic four-step with the KA LE BA SHI sequence of syllables. Concentrate on the order of the syllables and try to create your own rhythm over the four-step with the rhythmical elements of beat, off-beat and double off-beat, starting from the beginning after the fourth step. For example: first emphasize the syllable KA on the first step, then try emphasizing the syllable LE on step 2, then emphasize the syllables LE and BA on steps 3 and 4, and then BA on step 4. Next, try emphasizing these syllables by clapping your hands. After you develop a rhythm over one four-step, you can also try to develop a rhythm over two four-steps.

With this system of syllables, you can also learn all the time-line formulae, known by the terms clave, or guideline, which form the metric backbone in a piece of music (see Table 1.4).

4/4 Clave

Having described the first principles of rhythm, I will now explain the term clave in more detail. The clave forms the basis of African, Afro-Cuban and Afro-Brazilian music. Clave (which means "key") is a guideline which is usually played on two wooden sounding instruments, such as the "claves," or on bells, or sometimes on double bells. Played together with the drums, which often produce more complicated patterns and have a more muted sound, these small hand percussion instruments can be clearly heard due to their bright sound. They serve as a timekeeper. In the 4/4 clave, the basic pulse is subdivided into four beats. The whole ensemble—the drummers, singers and dancers, as well as the solo drummers—is based on the clave. The clave audibly penetrates the web of rhythmic drumbeats, and leads the musicians through the piece of music.

The four-part guidelines in Table 1.3 form the basis for many rhythms from different cultures. That is why good control of the clave certainly is a "key" for many rhythms.

In Africa, a very old drummer told me that the young drummers selected by a tribe first play the clave for several years before they are allowed to play the drum in an ensemble. This shows how important the control of the guideline is for African musicians; it is the rhythmic concept on which everything is based. An accompanist in salsa music also bases his compositions on the clave.

The choice of 4/4 clave patterns presented here are limited to those from Africa, Cuba, and Brazil. In Table 1.3, figure 2 shows the universal rhythm on which all other 4/4 claves are based, starting with the same basis as Table 1.2, figure 1. The 4/4 clave illustrated here describes the progress of five beats within a sequence of four rhythmic units (one unit being KA LE BA SHI), as shown in figures 3, 4 and 5.

In Cuba, figure 3 is described as the son-clave. This accompanying rhythm developed circa 1900 in the province of Oriente. The roots of salsa music lie in the son. This music was played with a guitar, bass (marimbula), bongos, maracas, voice, and several claves. The son clave is also the basic rhythm for other rhythms in this book.

Figure 4 shows the rumba clave, a development of the son clave. As you can see, the third beat, like the second beat, is on the syllable SHI. This produces a completely different feeling. The guaguanco rhythm, a specific form of rumba, is based on the rumba clave illustrated in figure 4.

Another clave that is often heard is the Brazilian clave known as the bossa clave, illustrated in figure 5. This 4/4 clave can be heard in the bossa nova, as well as in the Afro-Brazilian folk music from Bahia; it is also the root of other Brazilian guidelines.

Table 1.3: 4/4 Clave

	KA	LE	BA	SHI	KA	LE	BA	SHI	KA	LE	BA	SHI	KA	LE	BA	SHI	Pulse/Voice
Fig. 1	●				●				●				●				Feet
Fig. 2	●			●			●										Hands
Fig. 3	●			●			●				●		●				Hands
Fig. 4	●			●				●			●		●				Hands
Fig. 5	●			●			●				●			●			Hands

Claves are characterized by the division of a 4/4 bar into two bars. A bar is a unit of measurement that indicates divisions of rhythm and time in a piece of music. In principle, claves are two-bar rhythms. In the case of the son, rumba and bossa clave, this means that every 4/4 clave consists of a unit, or bar, of three beats and a unit of two beats (see pattern c), subdivided by the thick line into two large units. There is also a 3-2 clave. In addition, it is possible to have a 2-3 clave, if you start with the second unit (two beats) instead of the first unit (three beats). This is described in more detail in Part 5.

The rhythm in figure 2 forms the basis for all other guidelines. Beat, off-beat and double off-beat are represented here in a single rhythmic pattern. That is why it is important that figure 2 becomes a fixed part of your physical rhythmic consciousness. You should take plenty of time to practice the steps correctly, and then clap the different accents of figure 2 with your hands. If necessary, start by emphasizing only the syllable KA with the voice at first, later adding the syllables SHI and BA etc. You will discover the importance of this rhythmic pattern yourself, if you concentrate on listening to modern pop and rock music, and particularly the drums. You can hear the drummer's foot emphasizing or varying the accents of figure 2 or figure 3 with the bass drum.

The Value of Notes and Rests

Table 1.4 shows how the son clave shown in figure 3 of Table 1.3, which indicates the accents with dots, can be transcribed into musical notation. The columns presented in the tables serves to simplify the way in which the rhythm is shown. Normally, the only vertical lines in actual musical notation (other than those of the notes) are at the beginning and end of each bar, or joining different signatures that are played simultaneously by several different instruments or hands (as in musical notation for the piano). Rhythmic units developed known as "bars," contain the transcription of the notes. A 4/4 bar, as shown in Table 1.4, has note values of four quarter notes or eight eighth notes, or sixteen sixteenth notes, etc. There are equivalent rest values for all the note values.

For the notation of the son clave, I have chosen two possibilities both of which form the same rhythmic pattern. Two 4/4 bars, containing three horizontal lines, are used to notate the son clave correctly. This method of notation clearly shows the three emphases in the first bar and two emphases in the second bar. As was previously explained, this is a 3-2 clave. To present complicated compositions in a comprehensible way, it is a good idea to learn the rules of notation by heart. To help you read these, I have written the sequence KA LE BA SHI or U ME LA above every four- and three-beat rhythm in Part 5.

Table 1.4

Rhythmic Independence – 1

Table 1.5 shows another series of rhythm exercises aimed at developing a feeling for the independence of your right and left hand, and at the same time a sense of the interrelation between the movements of the left and the right side of your body. Drums such as the batá (see Part 5: Imbaloke) are suitable, in terms of appearance and sound, for playing the complex compositions of beats with the right and left hand.

It is a well-known fact that the left half of the brain controls the right half of the body. This part of the brain contains the center of rational thought, the intellect. The left half of the body is correspondingly controlled by the right half of the brain which is responsible for intuition, feeling, creativity and imagery. In some people, the right brain is dominant, and getting the right hand to cooperate may be difficult for them, while others who are left-brain dominant may have difficulty controlling the left hand. This polarity in our brain can be stimulated by rhythmic, physical work. It can help people to see things as a whole.

The patterns illustrated here should be seen as an example, and are of different degrees of difficulty. Choose the exercises which enable you to produce a flowing movement of the hands and feet, at your own tempo. Again, the four-step is the basis for the exercises. You say the sequence KA LE BA SHI so that you experience the regular pulse of four syllable units in four-steps. When your feet and voice work together as one, the accents of figure 1 (syllables BA, SHI) are produced lightly with your right hand on your right thigh or your torso. Figure 1 shows an important rhythmic stylistic element in African and Cuban music. In Part 5, this double off-beat is characteristic of the danza, kpacha, kpanlogo and tumbao rhythms.

When you feel that you have reached the limit of your ability, concentrate on figure 1 and clap the rhythm with two hands. If you want, you can then try figure 2, beating it with the left hand on the left thigh, along with figure 1. It will be some time before you have mastered the movements for both hands. The feeling that the right hand is doing something different from the left hand is quite exciting. At the same time, in these exercises, your body becomes used to having two rhythms going on at the same time. In order to play the two rhythms simultaneously, the exercises have to be done precisely. Figures 3-10 are practiced with your left hand, like figure 2, while your right hand continues with figure 1.

At the end of the learning process you can try to play the series of beats with your right and left hands on two drums or on a split drum. See what changes take place, now that the levels of rhythm and melody coincide.

What do you hear? How does the sound of the instrument influence the flow of your playing? After this, try to practice figure 1 with your left hand instead of your right hand, and all the other figures with your right hand. What has changed? What works, and what doesn't work? You will find that there are many interesting possibilities to practice, as well as lessons to be learned, in Table 1.5. The aim is to develop a physical rhythmic consciousness that allows in new possibilities of playing and expression in the concrete interaction with an instrument.

Table 1.5: Left and Right Hand

	KA	LE	BA	SHI	KA	LE	BA	SHI	KA	LE	BA	SHI	KA	LE	BA	SHI	Pulse
	●				●				●				●				Voice
Fig. 1			●	●			●	●			●	●			●	●	Feet
Fig. 2	●					●			●					●			Right Hand
Fig. 3	●						●		●						●		Left Hand
Fig. 4	●		●				●		●			●			●		Left Hand
Fig. 5	●		●			●					●		●				Left Hand
Fig. 6	●		●			●									●		Left Hand
Fig. 7	●					●	●	●						●		●	Left Hand
Fig. 8	●		●		●	●	●		●			●		●		●	Left Hand
Fig. 9	●		●			●			●				●		●		Left Hand
Fig.10	●			●			●				●		●				Left Hand

Rhythmic Independence – 2

The patterns in Table 1.6 are practiced in the same way as those in Table 1.5. In contrast with figure 1 in Table 1.5, figure 1 in Table 1.6 contains accents that correspond to the samba rhythm. The syllables SHI and KA are also emphasized with your right hand on your right thigh or on your torso.

Table 1.6: Right and Left Hand

	KA	LE	BA	SHI	KA	LE	BA	SHI	KA	LE	BA	SHI	KA	LE	BA	SHI	Pulse
	●				●				●				●				Voice
Fig. 1	●			●	●		●		●			●	●			●	Right Hand
Fig. 2			●		●							●	●				Left Hand
Fig. 3	●		●		●				●		●		●				Left Hand
Fig. 4		●		●		●	●			●		●		●	●		Left Hand
Fig. 5	●		●			●		●	●		●			●		●	Left Hand
Fig. 6	●		●			●		●		●			●		●		Left Hand
Fig. 7		●			●			●		●			●			●	Left Hand
Fig. 8	●			●			●			●			●				Left Hand
Fig. 9	●			●			●			●		●			●		Left Hand
Fig.10	●		●		●	●		●		●		●	●		●		Left Hand

2. Three-Beat Pulse

Table 2.1: Beat and Off-Beat

	U	ME	LA	U	ME	LA	U	ME	LA	U	ME	LA	Pulse/Voice
Fig.1	●			●			●			●			Feet
Fig.2		●			●			●			●		Hands
Fig.3			●			●			●			●	Hands

In the exercises up to now you have found how you can produce rhythmic lines with different beats in the four-beat pulse KA LE BA SHI. At the same time, this method enables you to gain an insight into the centuries-old understanding of rhythm in different cultures, which has had a great influence on modern music, such as pop and rock music; to loosely translate and African proverb: "The mother influences her children."

With a three-beat pulse, it possible to create ternary rhythms. For the three-beat pulse, I use the sequence of syllables U ME LA. This simple three-beat pulse forms the basis for many rhythms, such as the shuffle, swing, and also all 6/8 and 12/8 grooves. Like the KA LE BA SHI sequence, the sequence U ME LA is voiced with the basic four-step which you have already learned. As soon as you develop a flowing rhythm, you start to clap your hands to produce the emphases illustrated in figure 2 and then in figure 3. Notice how the physical feeling changes when you first clap the off-beat of the ME syllable and then the off-beat of the LA syllable, accompanying the basic rhythm of the feet. The conscious experience of clapping ME and LA off-beats is the exercise shown in Table 2.1. You have all the time in the world to familiarize yourself with the rhythmic energy of a three-beat pulse. The exercise in Table 2.1. also applies for Tables 2.2 through 2.6. When you have understood the beats and off-beats in the three-beat pulse, try this exercise: with the help of the four-step, try to create your own rhythmic pattern using the syllables, U ME LA, which starts from the beginning after the fourth step. The following exercise could be a rhythm on the basis of two four-steps. (See four-beat pulse, Table 1.2).

Polyrhythm

Polyrhythmic (from the Greek, "poly" meaning "many") tension is created by moving against the rhythm in two or more rhythmic series played at the same time, so that different rhythmic patterns are combined or cross over. This is also known as a cross rhythm. A simple example of an important cross rhythm is the simultaneous playing of two-beat and three-beat units within a single rhythmic cycle. Polyrhythmic structures form the basis of African music and are a musical part of many rituals and ceremonial practices.

Table 2.2 shows the 2:3 cross rhythm (figure 2), the 4:6 cross rhythm (figure 3) and the 4:3 cross rhythm (figure 4). Again, you use the syllables U ME LA and the four-step. When you are able to do this with the voice and feet, try to emphasize the syllables U and LA with the voice, before adding the syllable ME (see figure 2). When you think that you have mastered this, clap the accents illustrated in figure 2. The sounds of your feet and clapping of your hands produce the 2:3 cross rhythm with the right half of the body. The two-beat unit of the feet comes together with the three-beat unit of the hands in a single rhythmic cycle. On the other hand, it can also be said that the counter-rhythm of three claps dominates basic two-step meter. In this case, the rhythm is described as a 3:2 rhythm.

Figure 3 shows the 2:3 polyrhythm produced with the right as well as the left half of the body. In this case, six claps are played over four steps. This is also known as the 4:6 polyrhythm. Figure 4 explains the 4:3 polyrhythm. Here, a four-beat unit comes together with a three-beat unit in a single rhythmic cycle. This means that the three claps of the hands are played over the four steps of the feet. You will find these structures again in Part 5, in the section "Three-Part Rhythms" on the drums and bells. First, we will look at the exercises of the figures in Table 2.2.

Table 2.2: Polyrhythms

	U	ME	LA	U	ME	LA	U	ME	LA	U	ME	LA	Pulse/Voice
Fig.1	●			●			●			●			Feet
Fig.2	●		●	●									Hands
Fig.3	●		●	●			●		●	●			Hands
Fig.4	●			●					●				Hands

6/8 Clave

The three 6/8 claves illustrated here form the metric backbone of many 6/8 rhythms in the African, Afro-Cuban and Afro-Brazilian musical culture. It should be emphasized that the 2:3 rhythm is anchored in this pattern. The basic pulse is subdivided into three beats. Depending on the character of the piece of music, these are played at different tempos. The clave in figure 2 is the classic three-part guideline which supports many rhythms in ethnic music. The guideline in figure 2 is notated as 6/8 or 12/8, and is therefore known as the 6/8 clave or the 12/8 clave. It forms part of the drum music of the Santeria (see "Three-Part Rhythms – Imbaloke" on page 178). Figure 3 shows an African 6/8 clave, and Figure 4 shows a Cuban 6/8 clave, which you will encounter again in Part 5. Practice the 6/8 claves so that the accents indicated in the three-beat bar are first stressed vocally as you pronounce the syllables U ME LA, before you practice clapping them with the hands. Listen to the different rhythms of the various 6/8 claves and try to master them.

Table 2.3: 6/8 Clave

	U	ME	LA	U	ME	LA	U	ME	LA	U	ME	LA	Pulse/Voice
Fig.1	●			●			●			●			Feet
Fig.2	●	●		●	●		●			●		●	Hands
Fig.3	●	●		●				●		●			Hands
Fig.4	●	●				●		●		●			Hands

The Value of Notes and Rests

As in Table 1.5 of the chapter "Four-Beat Pulse," Table 2.4 shows the musical notation for the 6/8 clave of figure 2, Table 2.3. The six-part rhythm of this guideline needs two bars, i.e., twice six eighth notes or rests, to be notated. For a 12/8 rhythm, the bar line in the middle would disappear (see "Three-Part Rhythms – Gamamla" on page 174). In the first notation of the rhythm of the 6/8 clave, I have used only eighth notes and rests. It would also be possible to use quarter notes, but this is more difficult to illustrate graphically for a beginner. In the second example of musical notation, I have summarized the 6/8 clave in four groups of three. This notation clarifies the three-beat bar of U ME LA, and simplifies the way in which the rhythmic pattern can be shown in a system of notation. As I said for the four-beat pulse with regard to the sequence of syllables KA LE BA SHI, I used the U ME LA sequence of syllables for all the pieces of music with a three-beat pulse in Part 5. This makes it easier to learn the symbols for notes and rests used in European musical notation.

Table 2.4

Rhythmic Independence – 3

You can do the independence exercises for the right and left hand, based on the three-beat pulse of U ME LA, in the same way as you did for the four-beat pulse. Again, the exercises are merely examples which you can adapt for yourself. The right hand, which again claps the same constant rhythmic pattern, is the rhythmic stylistic element of the shuffle, a traditional element in boogie-woogie, blues, and rock-n-roll. The basic groove swings to the syllables LA and U. A light emphasis on 1, 2, 3, and 4 (i.e., the four U's) produces the right drive for the shuffle. If you are interested in shuffle music, listen to some of the old and new blues and rock-n-roll recordings. As I have said before, it all takes time, and I suggest that you start with the actual independence exercises only when your feet and right-hand shuffle (figure 1) are completely secure. It is not a matter of mastering everything all at once. Take your time to gradually incorporate the left hand. As you can see, figure 7 is a 6/8 clave. How do you experience the interplay of your right and left hand? Finally, try to play these rhythmic combinations on two drums or percussion instruments, and develop the exercises in your own way.

Table 2.5

	U	ME	LA	U	ME	LA	U	ME	LA	U	ME	LA	Pulse/Voice
Fig. 1	●			●			●			●			Feet
Fig. 2	●		●	●		●	●		●	●		●	Right Hand
Fig. 3	●					●	●					●	Left Hand
Fig. 4	●		●	●			●		●	●			Left Hand
Fig. 5	●	●		●	●		●	●		●	●		Left Hand
Fig. 6		●	●		●	●		●	●		●	●	Left Hand
Fig. 7	●			●			●		●		●		Left Hand
Fig. 8	●		●		●	●		●		●		●	Left Hand

Rhythmic Independence – 4

Table 2.6 concludes this section on the three-beat pulse. These exercises are carried out in accordance with the instructions in the previous independence exercises. However, this time, instead of your right hand beating the shuffle, it does the double off-beat of the three-beat pulse, which is also used as the stylistic element in a swing-tumbão, or in 6/8 tumbãos. Again, see how it feels to combine the 6/8 clave played with your left hand (figure 5) together with your right hand (figure 1). How do you experience the rhythmic interplay this time? Again, once you have mastered the exercises with your hands and feet, you can use drums or other percussion instruments to express the rhythmic tension and work out your own exercises.

Table 2.6

	U	ME	L A	U	ME	L A	U	ME	L A	U	ME	L A	Pulse/Voice
Fig. 1	●			●			●			●			Feet
Fig. 2		●	●		●	●		●	●		●	●	Right Hand
Fig. 3	●				●		●				●		Left Hand
Fig. 4	●		●		●		●		●		●		Left Hand
Fig. 5	●		●	●			●		●	●			Left Hand
Fig. 6	●		●		●	●		●		●		●	Left Hand

3. Five-Beat Pulse

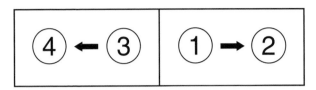

To expand your knowledge of many different rhythms, I would now like to draw your attention to the 2:5 cross rhythm. The 2:5 polyrhythm also consists of two rhythm cycles played at the same time. Five-part rhythms are found mainly in the musical culture of Southeast Asia and Eastern Europe.

To experience the 2:5 rhythm combination, you again need the well-known four-step as a basis. When you are able to do the steps in a flowing movement, start by singing one syllable with every step: KA with the first step, LE with the second step, BA with the third step, and SHI with the fourth step. It is important to do the steps at a fairly slow tempo and very evenly. After a while, the syllables can be omitted and a new rhythm of syllables develops on the basic steps. The steps are now combined with a pulse of five syllables: KA LE SHI BA SHI. When you start by pronouncing these syllables, it often happens that the four-part basic step becomes irregular. It might help to form an inner image of the sequence KA LE SHI BA SHI, before pronouncing it. It is important for the continuous four-step to remain flowing, so that you can feel the 2:5 pulse later on.

Table 3.1: Polyrhythm

	KA					LE					BA					SHI					Feet
	KA	LE	SHI	BA	SHI	KA	LE	SHI	BA	SHI	KA	LE	SHI	BA	SHI	KA	LE	SHI	BA	SHI	Pulse
Fig.1	•					•					•					•					Claps
Fig.2	•			•		•			•		•			•		•			•		Hands
Fig.3		•		•		•		•			•		•			•					Hands
Fig.4	•		•		•	•		•													Hands
Fig.5	•		•		•	•		•			•		•			•	•		•		Hands
Fig.6	•	•		•				•	•		•	•		•		•			•		Hands

When you get the syllables and steps going together well, you can start to work on the different figures shown in Table 3.1, which demonstrates the five-beat pulse in different ways, first by emphasizing the syllables with the voice, and then by clapping the hands. In figure 1, the steps are accompanied by a clap on syllable KA; in figure 2, the five-beat pulse of KA LE SHI BA SHI is subdivided with the hands into a three-beat and two-beat rhythm. This clearly shows how the combination of the number 3 and the number 2 can form a five-beat rhythm. Figure 3 invites you to accentuate the syllables LE and BA by clapping your hands. In the exercise shown in figure 4, you produce the 2:5 cross-rhythm on the right part of the four-step: four claps of the hands come together with the two steps with the right foot. In figure 5, the 2:5 cross rhythm is experienced both with the right and the left part of the four-step. Therefore it is also known as a 4:10 polyrhythm. Figure 6 gives an example of how it is possible to create your own rhythmic line with four KA LE SHI BA SHI sequences. Now try to play these rhythmic combinations on two percussion instruments, or to emphasize figure 1 with your feet while you use your hands to produce the accents of figures 2 and 5 on a drum. Of course, you can also create your own rhythms.

Part 5

Percussion Techniques and Rhythms

The Rhythms

Of the countless rhythms of the world's cultures, I have chosen those of African, Brazilian and Cuban music, because they are composed in such a way that they are interesting to learn, both for beginners and for more advanced players. Every rhythm comprises certain aspects of the exercises you have already practiced, and they are explained in further detail in the text. An explanatory guide and some background information will help you with creatively practicing the material shown in the musical notation.

The origin of the four-part and three-part rhythms presented here lies in African music, which was developed by the African slaves deported by the Spanish to Cuba, and by the Portuguese to Brazil, to produce different styles such as the rumba in Cuba and the samba in Brazil.

In Africa, music is one of the most important means of communication. In an article in 1928, Erich von Hombostel was the first music ethnologist to describe the three most important characteristics of African music: 1. antiphonal singing: a structure of call and response (alternating singing), which is found in gospel music, jazz, and in a modified form in pop music; 2. polyphony: two or more voices; 3. polyrhythms and strong syncopation as an expression of complex rhythms. African music is actually off-beat music. For people who are used to classical, European music, it is often difficult to understand this sort of rhythmic concept, because European music usually progresses in simple linear rhythmic structures.

When you study the rhythms, take plenty of time to play the different, so that you truly experience them. Practice is a matter of repetition. The inner dynamic and the strength of the rhythm lies in this regularity and repetition. This results in a change of time and space. When I play the rhythm for a long time, something in me starts to move, my feelings change, and I feel a sense of contentment. It's as if I am moving with the current, or flow, in time, in rhythm. The word rhythm comes from the Greek "to flow." Rhythm becomes tangible when the waves of pulsation, and of beat and off-beat are internalized, and this is accomplished through repetition.

From a musical point of view, every individual part of the group of figures which build up a rhythm is fairly easy to play. In fact, they are a reflection of the learning steps which were demonstrated in the previous section on the three-part and four-beat pulse. Practice at a tempo that allows you to consciously observe the different series of beats, so that you find it easier to understand the rhythm.

With regard to the instrumentation for the rhythms, I have used the conga, bata, djembé, kenkeni, doundoun, bells, campana and shékere, which represent very distinct musical styles, depending on how an ensemble is composed. For example, in Santeria music, the three sizes of the bata are used, while for the rumba, three congas of different sizes are used. The combination of different parts in a rhythm gives rise to impressive rhythmic patterns.

For me, drums and rhythms were the beginning of a path which brought me into contact with different cultures, different ways of thinking, and different people. Their influence has enriched my life and me as a person. Many stages in my musical and personal development are related to the rhythms presented here. It is my hope that these rhythms will open wonderful new possibilities for you, too.

The Conga Technique

As you already know, "conga" is a collective term for three types of hand drums which originate from Cuba. The three types of conga are: the tumba, (the large, low drum), the conga (the middle-sized drum), and the quinto (the small, yet tall, drum). You will come across the names of these drums in the Cuban and Brazilian rhythms in this chapter. For some examples of African music, the drums are described as the high, medium and bass drum, because these rhythms are normally played on African percussion instruments (i.e., kpanlogo drum), which also have a different sound. Of course, all African pieces of music can also be played on a conga set. The technique for playing the conga can easily be used for African drums, though the "floating hand" (see below) is primarily a Cuban and Brazilian style of playing.

The secret of powerful drumming with a rich sound lies in the mastery of a solid technique. This means that the basic strokes should be entirely understood to achieve the best control of the sound. It is only when you have mastered every stroke that you will be able to play powerful music. It is almost impossible to describe the technique for playing the conga in words, in any detail. The series of photographs on the following pages will therefore be much more useful than the descriptions on their own. It is important that you observe the different sound quality expressed by every stroke, so that you can develop this over time. A few lessons from an experienced conga player will make it much easier for you to learn to play this instrument.

Before starting on the exercises, make sure that you are sitting comfortably behind the congas. Your back should be straight, and your shoulders, arms and wrists should be relaxed, so that your arms are at an angle of about 90 degrees when you place your hands on the surface of the drum. It is important to have the right muscular tension in the hand beating the drum for every stroke. Never try to force the strokes. Make sure that you do not pull up your shoulders; they should be relaxed. Any muscular tension means that you are holding on, and will block the life energy flowing through you. Shaking your hands and arms will help to loosen and relax them. A few deep breaths, concentrating on breathing out, will help to remove any accumulated tension. When you are relaxed, it is easier to learn new things.

The Basic Strokes

We will go through the basic strokes with the help of the photographs.

First Basic Stroke
Open Stroke

This is an open stroke which produces a clear tone on the drum. The four fingers of one hand are stretched next to each other without being tensed. The whole surface area of your fingers strikes the skin of the drum. Choose a position so that the fingers strike the drum so that the back of the hand forms a line with the edge of the drum at the highest point. The movement of the stroke is made from the wrist. Touch the skin briefly so that the tone can ring out. With every stroke, make a subtle movement forwards with the fingers, noting how the sound changes. The more precisely this stroke is performed, the fuller the tone.

Second Basic Stroke
Bass Stroke

This basic stroke produces a muffled sound. It is made with the palm of your hand on the middle of the drum. The whole edge of your hand serves as an area of contact, so that the best possible contact is achieved between your hand and the skin of the drum. As a preliminary exercise, it is a good idea to drop the whole weight of the hand on the middle of the skin a few times. The bass sound can be heard by slightly tipping the drum.

Third Basic Stroke
Slap Stroke

This stroke produces a loud, hard tone. The slap stroke is the most difficult stroke on the drums. You need a great deal of patience before you get it to sound right. There is an introductory exercise that can give you an idea of the sound of the slap stroke. Place one of your hands on the drum in such a way that, seen from above, your wrist is held above the edge of the skin. Then the palm of your hand is raised, while your wrist stays in contact with the skin, and your hand strikes the skin. In performing this stroke, you concentrate on your fingertips, which stay in contact with the skin after you perform the stroke. If you do it correctly, your hand is placed in such a way that the edge of the drum runs under the back of your hand. The palm of your hand is slightly curved, and your fingers are relaxed. The slap stroke is also made from the wrist. It is important that your fingertips remain on the skin when they come down, and that the back of your hand goes back to the starting position. Try to practice this stroke without making too much effort.

Fourth Basic Stroke – Fingertip

This is a soft stroke with the fingertips on the drum. Your fingertips are used to play light strokes during the drumming, creating a flowing rhythm. For this technique, only your fingers are used, softly touching the skin. When you play tips, use them very lightly. Very little energy is used. A great deal of time and experience is needed to unobtrusively and professionally integrate tips in the drumming.

Fifth Basic Stroke – Whole Stroke

This produces a muffled sound. You make it with the whole ball of your hand on the middle of the skin. The stroke should not be made with too much pressure: keep your hand loose.

Sixth Basic Stroke
Whole Tip or Floating Hand

The whole tip, also known as the "floating hand," is a technique consisting of a whole stroke and a fingertip. The ball of your hand touches the skin alternately with your fingertips, resulting in a regular tilting movement. It is possible to start either with the ball of your hand (whole stroke) or with your fingertips (tip). It is important that while you are alternating the whole stroke and the tip, your hand is always in contact with the skin. The tilting movement should be very small.

Three other common basic strokes are the muffled slap and the muffled stroke, which are also described as muffled open and muffled tone, and the open slap. The muffled slap developed from the floating technique. Your left hand remains on the skin after a whole tip movement. Then your right hand performs the slap stroke. The muffled slap is easier than the normal slap stroke. This technique is used, for example, in the tumbao. The muffled open is played with the hand or with a stick. In Cuban drumming music, you can often hear the muffled open strokes during the virtuoso drumming of a quinto player. The muffled stroke played with a stick is found in the danza rhythm (see danza on page 162). For the open slap you do the same as for the normal slap, except that your fingers do not remain where they are after touching the skin. This stroke is found in the imbaloke rhythm, and also in djembé rhythms.

Like any other instrument, the drum can help you express and assimilate your inner feelings. When you have played the drum for a while, you will notice how your feelings change. The special quality of the conga is that the player makes direct contact with the skin, and therefore directly influences the sound. There is an immediate exchange of energy.

With your hands or fingers, try to get the skin to produce different sounds. Remember that the greatest vibrations are at the edge of the skin, where you will hear higher tones, i.e., more harmonics. When you strike the drum in the center of the skin, the lower tones are produced. During my lessons I use this exercise to confront the player with the sound energy aspect of the drum.

Every drum, large or small, round or slender, open or closed, has its own energy sound field. This forms the basis for the development of characteristic groups of instruments for particular styles. For example, samba music uses very different instruments from bata music.

Drumming is not merely a matter of technical skill: it affects a person as a whole—body, spirit and his soul.

Following is a summary of all the musical notes, signs for rests and other symbols which I have used for the notation of the different patterns given in the next section. The different parts in the rhythms that are described, which will be indicated in the patterns with figures 1, 2 etc., will be indicated in the text with line 1, line 2, etc.

Values of Notes and Rests

♩ = 1/2 note	♩ = 1/4 Note	𝄽 = 1/4 Rest
♪ or ♫ = 1/8 Note	𝄾 = 1/8 Rest	
♬ or ♬ = 1/16 Note	𝄿 = 1/16 Rest	
♪ = Grace Note	‖: :‖ = Repeat Sign	

Key for Signs

O = open stroke	S = slap stroke	B = bass stroke
T = fingertip	H = whole stroke	H-T = whole tip
Ø = muffled stroke	R = right hand	L = left hand
> = accent	↓ = start of the phrase	▲ = sign for the foot

The series of signs shown at the top right each set of rhythm notation indicate the tempo of the metronome (an instrument for indicating tempo and rhythm) for the rhythm concerned. If you set the metronome accordingly, you will hear the tempo of your foot. Strictly speaking, this is a 4/4 beat. However, for four-part rhythms, the foot always comes down on the first and third beat of every 4/4 bar.

Shékere

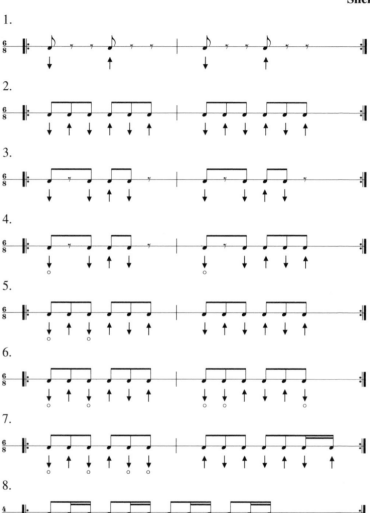

Symbol Legend:
↓ = movement of the shékere to bottom left – position 1
↑ = movement of the shékere to the right – position 2
0 = striking the bottom with the heel of the hand

The Shékere Technique

Before dealing with the actual rhythms, I would like to start by describing the technique of the shékere, because this instrument is used in a number of the following patterns.

You hold the shékere with both hands so that the open end points up. One hand (in this example, the right hand) lightly holds the neck, while the bottom rests in the palm of the other hand (position 1). When you move the shékere to the right, the instrument is in a horizontal position (position 2). The movement starts from your left hand and then your right hand actually moves the instrument. Then you return the instrument to position 1. This movement can be used to play many interesting rhythms.

Lines 1-7 give examples of rhythms with a three-beat pulse, which are suitable for playing in a 6/8 rhythm. The feeling for lines 3 to 7 develops automatically, with the basic exercises 1 and 2. The bead net should move evenly to and fro. An accompanying tone can be produced by striking the bottom with the heel of the left hand. This technique is used in lines 4-7. Line 8 shows a rhythm with a four-beat pulse. This is particularly suitable for the kpanlogo (see next page).

a. Kpanlogo

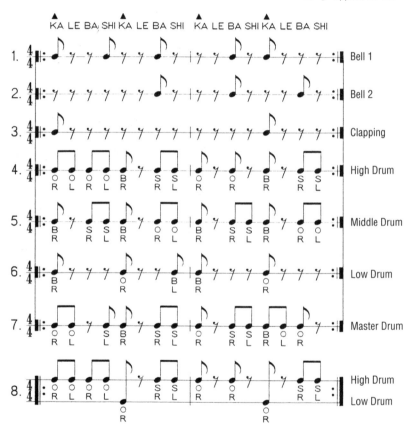

1. Four-Part Rhythms

Kpanlogo

The kpanlogo (pronounced "panlogo") is a rhythm from Ghana, which developed in about 1962. It involves dance, as well as singing and drumming. It is a simple rhythm, very suitable for a beginner, and is usually played by five to seven drummers. The sequence of syllables KA LE BA SHI shows where the accents lie in the four-beat pulse: as in every subsequent rhythm presented here, one foot is put down on the KA. When the syllable does not have a note value, the drum is not played.

Line 1 plus line 2 form the basis of the kpanlogo. Line 1, the son-clave, is played on a bell which produces a low sound (i.e., gonkogui or handbell) and line 2 is played with a high bell (e.g., cha-cha bell). Line 3 represents an elementary rhythm that you clap with your hands.

Now the drums. As you will see, there are three rhythm lines which are played on drums with a different pitch. When these are played together, the open strokes of the different lines form a melodic structure. The master drummer plays the basic pattern (line 7) over this. The master drummer is the soloist who plays variations which are related to specific dance movements. The pitch of the master drum should contrast with the sound of the three other drums. Make sure that the basic strokes are performed correctly, so that the open strokes can be clearly heard.

Line 8 shows how one player can perform two drum patterns at the same time, and thus accompany the master drummer very effectively. For this purpose, the high and low drum are placed next to each other, and instead of playing the bass stroke in line 4, the drummer plays an open stroke on the low drum with the right hand. The melody of the kpanlogo rhythm is maintained in this way.

The shékere is an important instrument in many African rhythms. It supports the flow of the rhythm and metaphorically "oils" the music. A typical shékere pattern for the kpanlogo is illustrated in line 8 of the shékere pattern on page 156. This part can also be played with the cabasa, caxixi, or tambourine.

b. Kpacha

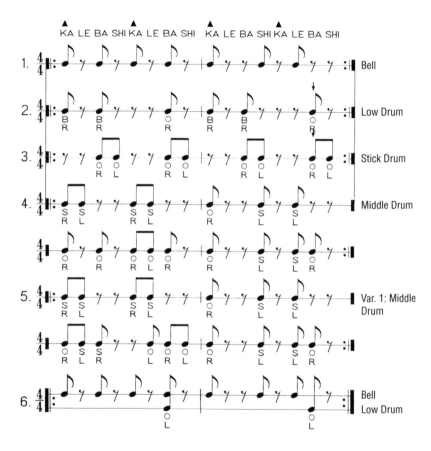

Kpacha

Kpacha is the name of this quick rhythm from West Africa (Ghana). Traditionally, it is performed every year in the Ga-Adangba region by boys and girls of marriageable age. Wise men pass on the rights and duties to the younger generation when they are initiated into adulthood.

The kpacha is a rhythm for four players. It is only when all the parts play together perfectly that the kpacha reveals its enchanting power. Lines 1, 2 and 3 form the rhythmic foundation for line 4, the main part. As you can see, line 3 is played on a drum with a stick. The accents are alternately placed with the right and left hand, with two drumsticks. Use wooden drumsticks and hold them so that the thick end strikes the skin when you are playing. In this position you can make better use of the repeat stroke. The drum should be tuned in between the middle and the low drum. It is important to strike the off-beats on the drum with the sticks in the correct rhythm. The same applies for line 4, the master part. Only in this way can you clearly hear the rhythmic alternation of beat and off-beat strokes which is so characteristic of the kpacha. Like line 5 (master variation 1), line 4 also covers four bars. Line 6 shows how a single player can combine the part of the bell (line 1) with line 2. The bell should be firmly secured to a drum or stand. With your right hand (stick) you place the accents of the bell's part, and at the same time, you play the open stroke on the low drum (tumba) with your left hand. In this way it is possible to perform the whole rhythm with three players. Concentrate on what it feels like to do two things at once on a bell and a drum.

c. Danza

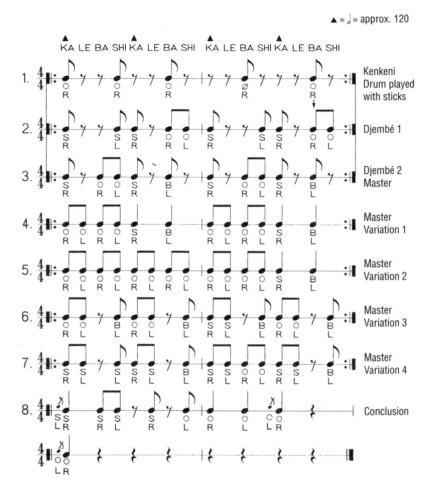

Danza

The danza comes from Mali, and is played by the Griots of the Kasonka tribe to accompany their dances. It is a fast, lively rhythm played by at least three drummers on traditional djembé drums, with their fascinating high clear tones and full bass tones.

As you can see, there is no pattern for the bell, but in its place there is a bass drum (kenkeni) which is struck with a stick, serving as a clave. The important thing about this basic rhythm (line 1) is the muffled stroke in the second bar. To do this, press the stick firmly against the skin after the stroke. Line 1 corresponds to the clave rhythm of the kpanlogo.

Line 2 accompanies the master part without any variations. With the accent on the four in the second bar, it acts as a support for the many variations of the master part. Line 2 uses only open and slap strokes.

Line 3 forms the basis for the master part. The open strokes alternate attractively with the open strokes of the support part. The series of strokes in line 3 allows the drummer to develop the different variations illustrated in lines 4, 5, 6 and 7. To achieve the best effect, the basic master part comes back from time to time and is then varied again. Later on, your own improvisations will provide even more musical expression.

Line 8 is the traditional final pattern which concludes the rhythm. As soon as this series of strokes is played, all the players know that the music is coming to an end, or—depending on what has been arranged—that other music is being introduced. The double stroke in line 8 is a special element. The grace note, also known as a preliminary stroke, serves to give the main stroke a more dense and, therefore, more powerful sound. This element for phrasing is also suitable for improvisations: it adds color and appeal to the drumming. You play it by striking the drum skin with both hands, so that one hand is higher than the other; your hands strike the skin, one just after the other.

d. Guaguanco – Part 1: Exercises

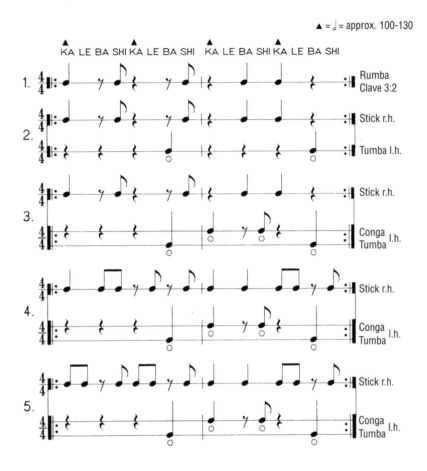

Guaguanco – Part 1

The guaguanco (pronounced "wah-wan-ko"), a four-part rhythm, is a traditional rumba. In Cuba, there are three important rumba rhythms: the yambu, the columbia, and the guaguanco. These differ in terms of their rhythm and style of dancing. The guaguanco consisted of anecdotes in a poetic (sung) form. Later this developed into the dance (rumba de guaguanco). This dance, which is performed by one dancer or a number of couples, is characterized by erotic gestures and movements, depicting the approaches between men and women, conquest and rejection. In the percussion ensemble the most important instruments are the quinto and the tumbadoras (congas), a few claves, on which the singer plays the clave beat, and the pallitos (wooden sticks).

Before describing the actual drumming patterns in Part 2, I would first like to give you some technical exercises that will help you develop your coordination so that you can learn to play the rumba clave and cascara parts accurately. In addition, these exercises will show how the characteristic guaguanco melody, the rumba clave and the cascara lines intermingle. The cascara is usually played with two wooden sticks on a bamboo tube, a woodblock or a timbales barrel (also known as a paila).

With Exercise 1, you will become familiar with the rumba clave. You play this clave by striking the metal parts or the wall of the barrel of the tumba with a stick in your right hand. Note the difference from the son clave!

Exercise 2 shows how to combine the clave with the open strokes of the tumba. If you maintain the tempo is with your feet, make sure that the open strokes can be clearly heard in the off-beat.

Exercise 3 completes the guaguanco melody by developing the drumming of your left hand on a second instrument, the conga. Your right hand continues to practice playing the rumba clave. Concentrate on the different movements of your left and right hand.

Exercises 4 and 5 show how the cascara parts are played together with the guaguanco melody on the conga and the tumba. First, practice the cascara part with your right hand. Start by playing the open strokes on the tumba with your left hand, and later add the open strokes on the conga. Again, concentrate on the separate movements of your hands.

Once you have mastered the rhythmic tension of the rumba clave, you will be able to increase the independence of your right and left hand with another exercise. Playing with both hands, first try to add vocal emphasis on the accents that would be played with your right hand, and then try vocalizing the accents of the left hand.

d. Guaguanco, Part 2

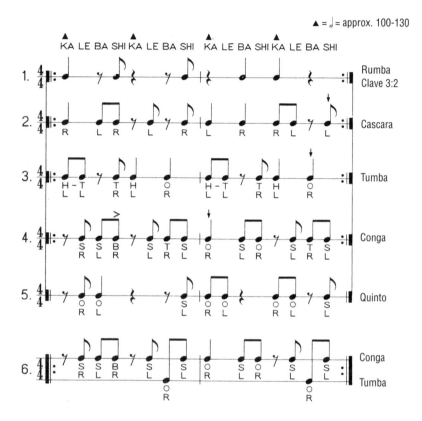

Guaguanco – Part 2

As you see in the notation of the true guaguanco rhythm, five players are needed to play this rhythm. In addition to the rumba clave (line 1) and the cascara part (line 2), there are parts that are played on the tumba and the conga. As soon as players 1 and 2 can maintain a flowing rhythmic interplay of the clave and the cascara parts, player 3 (line 3) joins in with the tumba on the open stroke on beat 4 of the second bar. Then, player 4 (line 4) joins on the conga on the first beat of the second bar. It is important to play the slaps fairly softly so that the open strokes can be clearly heard.

Line 5 shows the characteristic accents for playing the quinto. This is played as a solo instrument. If the tumba and conga are played by one drummer, only the fingertip of the conga part has to be replaced by the open stroke of the tumba (line 6). Listen to recordings on which you can study the rumba music of Cuban folklore.

e. Samba

Samba

The word "samba" reminds most people of the large batucadas which pass through the streets of Rio de Janeiro during the carnival. The traditional samba schools such as Manguera, Portela, or Padre Miguel, developed in the late 1920s from the organization of district carnival groups. By the end of the nineteenth century, carnival music was strongly influenced by Europe. It was only in the second half of the twentieth century that Afro-Brazilian music took the place of European music, and samba became the symbol of Brazilian music. Since that time, classical samba instruments such as the surdo, ganza, agogo, caixa etc., have determined the sound of the samba orchestra to an important extent, but the samba's fiery character can also be heard when it is played on congas.

The drum parts shown here contain certain rhythmic motifs that are characteristic of different styles of samba music. The samba swings in a four-part rhythm, which corresponds to the sequence of syllables KA LE BA SHI. In this case, a sequence corresponds to the four sixteenth notes in a quarter note. The separate parts are not difficult to play in themselves. However, the rhythmic phrasing required for samba music is difficult. The samba has a pulse of 4 x 4 sixteenth notes, which are accented with different emphases. The voice exercise in line 1 shows the main accents in a basic form of the samba. You can practice this basic rhythm with your voice, using the sequence of syllables TA KA CHI KA, starting with the accent on the KA (before the first beat).

Lines 2 and 3 are samba patterns, which are played on a conga. They are taken from the traditional samba de roda, played in the sugar cane areas of Salvador. For the correct phrasing of lines 2 and 3, first listen to some traditional samba music, in which you hear the "balancado," where the sixteenth notes are played between a binary and a ternary feeling. To become familiar with the feeling of samba music, it's a good idea to start by playing the voice exercise in line 1 on the conga.

Line 4 is derived from the "samba partido alto" style, which was influenced by the samba forms from Bahia. The partido alto always has a funky sound and is extremely popular in the old shanty towns of Rio de Janeiro.

The drum patterns in lines 5, 6, and 7 are played on a conga and a tumba. They also use the "floating hand" technique. Lines 5 and 7 are samba patterns from the "samba de enredo." Line 6 is a samba-salsa mixture, which is also suitable for pop, funk, or salsa music.

Rhythmic Independence 5 – Drums

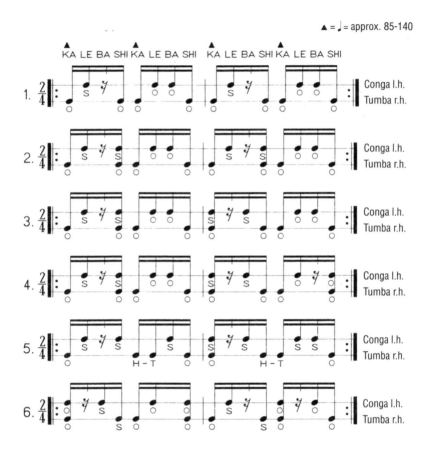

Rhythmic Independence 5 – Drums

This exercise explores the independent playing of the left and right hand on two drums in greater detail. Table 1.6 of Part 4 (Rhythmic Independence 2), in which the first samba accent was practiced, serves as a basis for this.

In line 1, your right hand plays the classical samba accent, while your left hand plays a simple rhythmic pattern. The technique for your right hand stays the same for all the exercises, except the exercises in lines 5 and 6. The playing with the left hand is constantly developed with dense rhythmic accents resulting in a traditional tambourim part (in line 4). This shows two rhythmic patterns progressing independently of each other, producing a strong rhythmic tension.

When you are practicing, you can try to combine the different bars of the left hand. For example, bar 1 in line 1 can be combined with bar 2 in line 2. All the rhythms in lines 1-4 can be incorporated in the groove of a samba batucada. These patterns are especially suitable for a fast tempo. Line 5 shows how this technique can be further developed. In Brazil, this sort of samba drumming is known as "samba de caboclo." As in Cuba, it also uses the floating hand technique. Line 6 shows the combination of the "samba de roda" and that of the "partido alto" rhythm.

a. Bembé

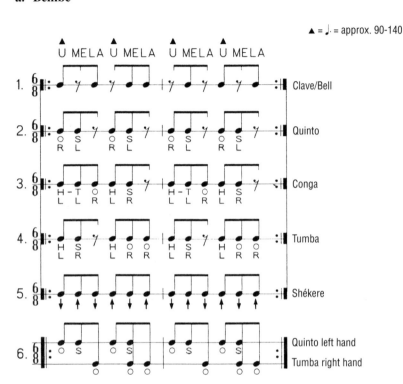

▲ = ♩. = approx. 90-140

↓ = movement of shékere to bottom left

↑ = movement of shékere to the right

2. Three-Part Rhythms

Bembé

The bembé, an Afro-Cuban rhythm for five players, is played on festive occasions that are also known as bembé. It is played on drums with different pitches to build up a melodic line, which serves as a recurring theme. In this melody, variations are drummed to underline the movements of the dancers. The high conga (quinto) is known in the Afro-Cuban tradition as the "katchimbo", the middle one is known as the "mula" and the tumba is known as the "caja."

Over the course of time, with the merging of different cultures, different styles and techniques have developed for the bembé. One of the possibilities is illustrated in lines 1 to 5, where the bembé is played on a bell, three drums and a shékere. The 6/8 clave is the basic rhythm of all the drum parts. Therefore the bembé swings in a 6/8 rhythm, in the three-part U ME LA pulse. In this rhythm, like the following rhythms, it is important to make sure that every syllable U is marked with the foot. Line 2 shows a quinto pattern with an open stroke on every first and fourth eighth note. In line 3, the pattern for the middle conga, the open tone comes on the third eighth note of every bar. In line 4, the tumba pattern, your right hand plays the open strokes on the fifth and sixth eighth notes. When lines 2, 3, and 4 are played together, they form a compact melodic line which swings in a 2:3 cross rhythm. The three-beat pulse of the 6/8 rhythm is clearly emphasized with the shékere in line 5. Line 6 serves as an example and an inspiration to play the bembé on a conga and a tumba at the same time. Your left hand constantly plays the accents of line 2, while your right hand independently plays the open strokes of lines 3 and 4. Try to create your own bembé variation with the help of the notation given for the conga and tumba.

b. Gamamla

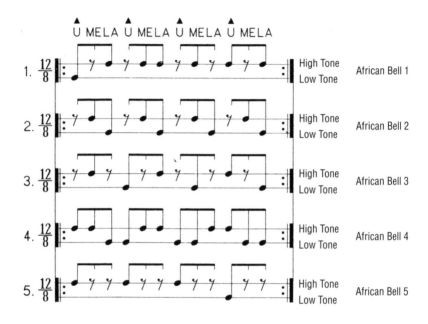

▲ = ♩. = approx. 65-100

Gamamla

This special piece for African bells in ewe-beat is popular in Ghana, and is reminiscent of the Balinese gamelan orchestra. The gamamla reveals that rhythm also has aspects of melody. The parts are played on bells in different rhythms, and are built up on the basic pattern of the 12/8 bell (pattern 1), interrelating in such a way that melodic lines are created.

This rhythm is a concrete transposition of the off-beat and pulse exercises in the three-beat pulse in Part 4. There are five parts for bells, usually played on the African double bells (gonkogui). You press the bass bell against your stomach or thighs after you strike it; this technique produces a sound with a very special timbre. You can also use other instruments, such as temple blocks, or woodblocks in different sizes. The combination of wooden and metal bells also produces attractive mixtures of sounds. For example, you can use rubber or felt beaters, as well as the more commonly used wooden sticks, to produce softer nuances of sound.

In this piece of music, line 1 shows the 12/8 ewe-beat clave, which is crossed by three other bell parts. In this, line 2 contains the off-beat of the three-part pulse. You can feel the tension of the 2:3 cross rhythm in line 3. This part is considered the most difficult because of the way in which the high and low tones alternate. When playing line 4, it is desirable to incorporate rests, so that the other bell parts can be heard.

If you want to practice this rhythm on your own, you can first record line 1 on a cassette recorder, and then play the other parts to accompany it.

Once you have mastered the material, you can try to create new parts for the bells yourself, or compose your own piece. The rhythmic patterns of the gamamla serve as an excellent inspiration for your own improvisations, whether these are played on the bells, or on another instrument, such as the conga.

c. **Fume-Fume**

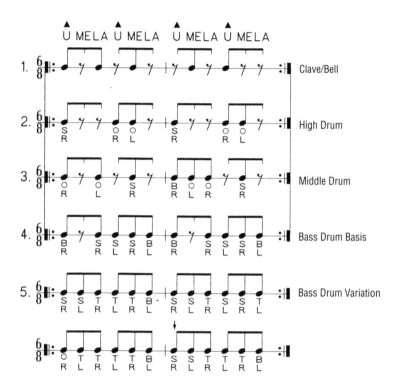

Fume-Fume

This three-part rhythm from Ghana was originally dedicated to bringing in the harvest and was developed with further compositions by the African musician and master drummer, Mustapha Tettey Addy.

The fume-fume is based on the sequence of syllables U ME LA, and is played on three drums and a bell. The special musical characteristic of the fume fume is that in this rhythm the 6/8 clave has a different form from the bembé or gamamla. This 6/8 clave was presented in Part 4 in the section on three part rhythms, Table 2.3. It is clear that the accents in this 6/8 clave also appear in the bembé or the gamamla. Lines 2 and 3 show two drum patterns that serve to accompany the rhythm here. The two lines together create the 2:3 cross rhythm, which can be clearly identified in the first bars. When practicing lines 2-5, to create the right rhythmic tension, make sure that the drum parts can be clearly heard in relation to the 6/8 bell in line 1. Lines 4 and 5 present the master part on the bass drum with a variation.

With regard to the feet, after dividing the fume-fume into four steps, you can try to place your feet only on the first and third U of the U ME LA pulse; in this way the whole rhythm is divided into only two steps. This may be rather difficult at first, but you will soon see that the rhythm starts to flow in a completely different way, which is closer to the rhythmic tension of the fume-fume. This becomes very clear in the dance: the basic step of the fume-fume corresponds with the first and third syllable U. This feeling is supported by the bass strokes in pattern 4 (always the first beat of the 6/8 bar). With this new metric arrangement, there are twice as many off-beats in every bar in the three-beat pulse.

d. Imbaloke

▲ = ♩. = approx. 110-125

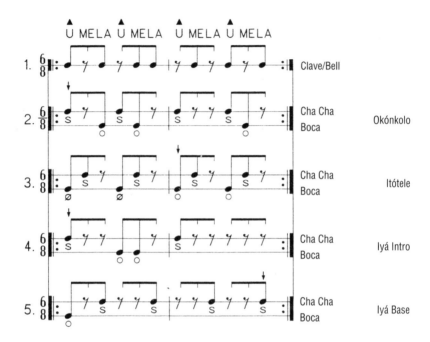

Imbaloke

Along with the "cha-cha-roch-a-fu," the imbaloke is one of the rhythms known as party toques. These are patterns which accompany the songs of the different gods, rather than being devoted to one particular god. The imbaloke rhythm is played on the batá, which are drums with two surfaces that have different pitches: the small "cha-cha" and the large "boca." The player sits, resting the drum on a thigh, with a belt or strap around the legs or upper body to stop the drum from sliding away; this allows the player to use both hands, with a sideways movement. The left hand plays the cha-cha, the right hand the boca.

Because of the different sizes of the drum surfaces, different pitches are produced. The "okónkolo" vibrates as a whole in a higher frequency range than the thick "iyá." It is best to stretch the skins of the bata drums tautly, particularly those of the cha-chas, to produce a high sound; this is actually the secret of the unique sound that entrances uninitiated spectators.

Four players are needed for the imbaloke, and the rhythm moves in the three-beat pulse of the 6/8 bell. Without exception, the patterns of okónkolo, itótele and iyá (toques) are played with a 6/8 feeling. All the cha-chas are played with open strokes. The bocas of the okókolo and the itótele are played with open strokes, and sometimes with muffled open strokes, and the open stroke for the okónkolo is played with only three fingers. The iyá, the mother of all drums, is played as a bass stroke with the whole hand. The strokes should be placed close to the edge of the skin. The iyá opens with the pattern in line 4 (intro.). Then the okónkolo and the itótele join in. Later, the iyá switches to its own pattern (line 5). It is interesting to see how the cha-chas produce an even pattern of sounds when they play together, while the clear, open strokes of the okónkolo and the itótele, and the full bass tone of the iyá can also be heard. This results in a dense pattern of drumbeats.

e. Mandjiane

$\blacktriangle = \downarrow. = $ approx. 80-120

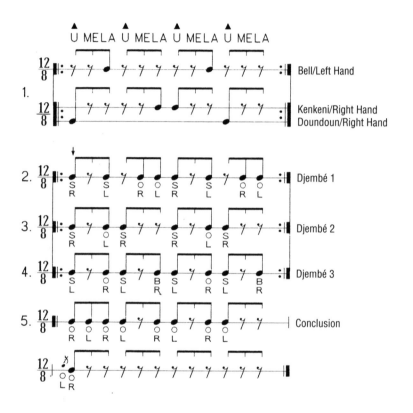

Mandjiane

This interesting-sounding rhythm from Guinea is the last in the series of three-part rhythms. It is said that the mandjiane is played in Guinea, accompanied by the acrobatic tricks of young girls, at the fish-catching festival.

Four players are needed for this rhythm. As for the danza rhythm, djembés and bass drums are used, but in the mandjiane, a bell (such as a "doundoun" bell), a second bass drum, the doundoun, and a third djembé are added to the traditional danza instruments.

Line 1 forms the basis of this rhythm which consists of three parts: one for bell and two for bass drums. The bell is attached to one of the drums. The player's right hand strikes the kenkeni and doundoun with a thick stick, while the left hand hits a bell with a thin stick. The player decides where to start in pattern 1: for example, with either the first stroke on the kenkeni, or the second stroke on the doundoun. The listener will experience the rhythm in a completely different way every time. It is important for the players to understand the way in which the parts interconnect, and for them to feel the three-part pulse.

When the player of line 1 has established a rhythm, the next player starts at the beginning sign of line 2 using sharp, open slaps (the fingertips do not remain on the skin). Like line 2, line 3 has the function of an accompanying drum. Line 4 should be played on a fairly large djembé so that the bass strokes can be heard clearly. Essentially, this drum part plays the basic pattern of a shuffle rhythm. In order to make the rhythm more varied, every djembé player, depending on his experience and skill, can play a solo. To end the solo in a way that is clear for the other players, play line 5. This pattern generally serves to introduce the end of the rhythm. It is important for the drummer to play the final pattern accurately and with emphasis, so that it is clearly understood by the whole ensemble, and the other players can respond correctly. It takes a great deal of time and practice to master this task.

Tumbao Rhythms

a. Tumbao

Conga

b. Swing Tumbao

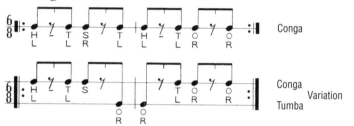

Conga

Conga   Variation

Tumba

c. Rock-Pop Tumbao

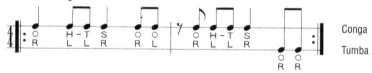

Conga

Tumba

d. 9/8 Tumbao

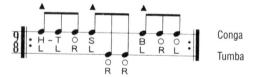

Conga

Tumba

e. 5/4 Tumbao

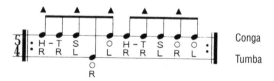

Conga

Tumba

f. 7/4 Tumbao

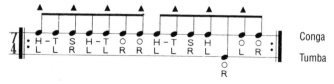

Conga

Tumba

3. Tumbao Rhythms

The tumbao forms the basic rhythm of the conga and is derived from the tumbadora (the Cuban version of an African drum), an important instrument in Afro-Cuban music. The tumbadora and the "tambores de conga" are the precursors of our conga, and were used in early Cuban carnival music ("conga de comparsa"). Although slavery was abolished in Cuba in about 1880, the racism that persisted prevented the tumbadora from being allowed in dance halls. From the second half of the nineteenth century, the tumbadora formed the backbone of the two most important forms of Afro-Cuban music: the rumba and the conga. Later on, other well-know rhythms such as the son montuno, the cha-cha-cha and the mambo were developed.

The tumbao (figure a.) as the basic rhythm of the conga is characterized by two open strokes on the last two eighth notes of the bar. All the tumbao rhythms presented here have this characteristic, with the exception of the swing tumbao (figure b.), which is the only one with a three-beat pulse, played in ternary style or triplets. This technique is very suitable for jazz or shuffle music. Figure c. shows the tumbao pattern for rock and pop songs played on the conga and tumba. In fact, this rhythm illustrates the main accents of a bass drum (open strokes) and a snare (slap strokes), which are commonly played on a rock music drum kit, though in a simplified form.

Figures d-f clearly show that a tumbao can also be played with an uneven rhythm. Special attention should be paid to the signs for the feet. The combination of the foot (beat), and the different tumbao patterns clearly reveal the dynamic tensions of a 9:8, 5:4 or 7:4 tumbao. All the tumbao patterns presented here are meant to inspire you to think of your own variations.

Rhythms for Two Drums and Clave

a. Palo

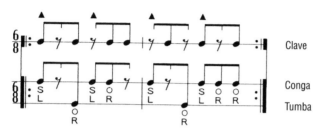

b. Columbia

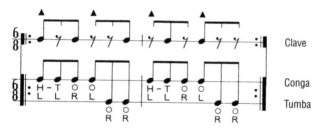

c. Bossa Nova

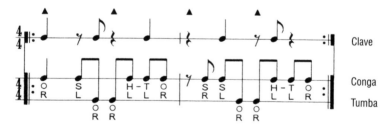

4. Rhythms for Two Drums and Clave

Traditional rhythms can also be played on two congas. Therefore, I have provided three additional rhythms here, to be studied by two players. If you are drumming on your own, you can sing the clave with the drum parts, which is a very effective exercise for improving your understanding of the interaction of the clave and the rhythm. In addition, you learn to do two things at once: drumming and speaking or singing.

Line a shows a rhythm which, like the makuta and the yuka, originates from the Congo cycle. (Congo is a religion of African origin.) The palo describes the atmosphere which prevails when people are working in the Cuban fields, cutting sugar cane with large knives. The melodic line of the palo, which was originally played on a number of different drums, is brought together here for the conga and the tumba.

The columbia, which has a 6/8 rhythm, is played very quickly, and feels as though it is played between the binary and ternary rhythms. Like the yambu and the guaguanco, the columbia belongs to the group of rumba rhythms.

The bossa nova, which developed from samba music, was popularized in the 1950s by musicians such as Joao Gilberto and Stan Getz. The rhythm is rather cool with understatements in the expression, and becomes alive in the harmonious chord changes. Several jazz standards, such as *Blue Bossa* or *One Note Samba*, are played in a bossa rhythm. The bossa nova clave, characteristic of this musical form, is usually played by the percussionist with a stick on the edge of the snare (rim shot), while the bass drum emphasizes the classic samba accents. In principle, these strokes are played with open strokes in the conga part.

Rhythms for Two Drums, Clave and Campana

a. Mambo

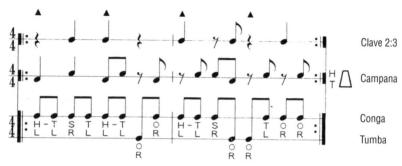

b. Son Montuno

5. Rhythms for Two Drums, Clave and Campana

The campana, also known as the hand bell or bongo bell, plays an important role in Afro-Cuban music. It is usually played by a bongocero (bongo player). It is a cowbell with a low sound, which you should play so that the bell lies flat in your left hand, while the open end of the instrument points away from your body. Your index finger of your left hand rests on the bottom of the cowbell, while your thumb and other fingers firmly hold the instrument. In addition, you can mute the sound with your index finger, or make it more open by removing it. You strike the campana with a thick wooden stick, but you can also play it with different mallets, to produce a softer sound. There are two ways of playing the campana in the exercises shown here. You can hit the wooden stick against the rim of the opening with your right hand for a deep, full sound, or you can hit the bottom part of the bell, near the welded end, for a sharp sound. It is important that these two sounds are distinct when they are played so that the contrast in the rhythmic phrasing is clearly expressed. The campana has been shown in the margin in the notation.

Here are some examples of rhythms: the clave is the basis and therefore the most important rhythmic component. As you know, the clave beat serves as a guideline with a structure of two bars. This means that certain accents fall on the first or second bar. The son clave (4/4 clave) in the 3:2 form is found in the son montuno (line b). In the 2:3 form it is played in the mambo (line a). All the other parts, such as the campana or conga parts which also consist of two bars, should be subordinate to the interpretation of the clave. It is only with the correct combination of clave, campana and congas that the specific Cuban tonality and its rhythmic tension can develop.

The mambo and son montuno belong to the predominantly urban musical style of the "salsa" (sauce). The roots of popular salsa music lie in the "son," which combines African and Spanish elements to form a whole. The son developed toward the end of the 19th century in Oriente, an Eastern province of Cuba. In a traditional rural son group, the singer is accompanied by a guitar with three strings (known as a tres). The bass part is played by a marimbula and a botja (oil bottle) with an opening on the side. In 1920, the son also reached the towns of Cuba. The mambo combines elements of the son in its rhythms and adds color to many pop recordings.

The classical salsa band (or conjunto band), which developed in about 1940, consisted of a wind section, piano, bass, and vocalists. There was also a percussion of congas, bongos, timbales, claves and maracas. The arrangement of a salsa piece consists of various alternating parts. For example, the montuno part, which is alternately shared by the choir and a soloist, and the bongo player transferring to the campana (hand bell), are characteristic of a salsa composition.

The mozambique (c) is related to the conga de comparsa (d). This was developed by the Cuban percussionist, Pelle el Afrokan. The two rhythms both have the same clave which is familiar to you from the rumba (guaguanco), as a basis. A 3:2 clave is used instead of a 2:3 clave. Both rhythms have been presented in a simplified form here, adapted for a small combo of three players. For the traditional mozambique and conga de comparsa, many congas are used. Thus many drums, as well as the full bell sounds, form the backbone of a conga de comparsa in a Cuban carnival, which is dominated by music and dance. The streets are full of thousands of people pulsating to the sounds of drums and bells of the comparsa. The rhythms of the processions through the streets were later introduced into the dance halls in Cuba, where they were picked up by the conjuntos and combined with their own style. In this way, rhythms related to the comparsa, such as the mozambique, were developed.

c. Mozambique

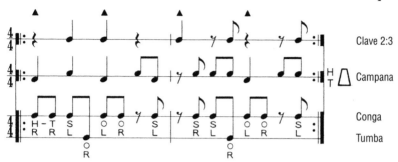

Clave 2:3

Campana

Conga

Tumba

d. Conga de Comparsa

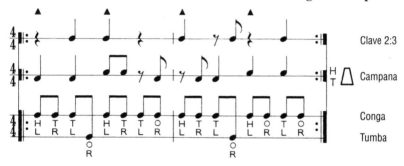

Clave 2:3

Campana

Conga

Tumba

Appendix

Discography

Mustapha Tettey Addy. *Les Percussions du Ghana*, Arion, 1994, CD 64055.

———. *Master Drummer from Ghana*, Lyrichord, 1992, CD 7250.

King Sunny Ade. *Live at the Hollywood Palace*, Cema/I.R.S., 1994, CD 29363.

Australian Aboriginal Music – Didjeridoo, Playa Sound, 1996, CD 65167.

Ray Barrett.o *Ancestral Messages,* Concord Picante, 1993, CD 4549.

Sergio Boré. *Intuicao*, Instinct, 1997, CD 358.

———. *Tambores Urbanos*, Instinct, 1995, CD 325.

Xavier Cugat and His Orchestra. *Cuban Mambo*, La Mejor Musica, 1997, CD 50310.

Paulinho Da Costa. *Agora,* Original Jazz Classics, 1991, CD 630.

Adama Dramé. *Mandigo Drums,* Playa Sound, 1994, CD 65085.

———. *30 Years of Jembe*, Playa Sound, 1997, CD 65177.

Gamelan Semar Pegulingan, World Music Library, 1994, CD 5180.

Grupo de Capoeira Angola Pelou. *Capoeira Angola from Salvador Brazil*, Smithsonion/Folkways, 1996, CD 40465.

Mickey Hart. *Planet Drum*, Ryko Gold Records, 1994, 24K Gold Disc CD 80206.

———. *At the Edge*, Ryko, 1990, CD 124.

Kodo. *Heartbeat Drummers of Japan,* Sheffield Lab, 1996, 24K Gold Disc CD 10507.

———. *Ibuki*, Tristar Music Imports/Sony Music Entertainment, Inc., 1997, CD 36852.

Fela Anikulapo Kuti. *Mr. Follow Follow*, Terrascape, 1997, CD 4002.

Airto Moreira. *The Other Side of This*, Ryko, 1992, CD 10207.

———. *Free*, Sony, 1988, CD 40927.

Eddie Palmieri. *Lucumi Macumba Voodoo-Lengendas*, Sony Discos, 1995, CD 81530.

Tito Puente. *Cuban Carnival*, BMG/International, 1991, CD 2349.

Mongo Santamaria. *Afro Roots,* Prestige (Fantasy), 1997, CD 24018.

Ravi Shankar. *Chants of India*, Emd/Angel, 1997, CD 55948.

———. *The Sounds of India*, Sony, 1987 CD 9296.

Gary Thomas. *Didgeridoo,* Aquarius, 1996, CD 10.

Glen Velez. *Rhythmcolor Exotica*, Ellipsis Arts, 1996, CD 4140.

———. *Handdance*, Nomad, 1996, CD 50301.

Resources

Ready to buy an instrument? Here's a short list of some companies who carry many of the instruments in this book. If you can connect to the Internet (by your own or someone else's computer), you'll find a wealth of information about drums and percussion instruments. To speed up your search, try typing the following URL in your browser "Go to:" window:
http://www.yahoo.com/Business_and_Economy/Companies/Music/Instruments/Percussion/
OR you can try these selected sites, send email, or phone, fax or write for information:

All One Tribe® Drum
Beautiful ceremonial drums made by master Native American
drummakers Henry Samora, Paul Concha and Del Romero from Taos
Pueblo.
P.0. Drawer N
Taos, New Mexico 87571
http://artsantafe.com/allonetribe/drums.html
1-800-442-DRUM (3786)
or Email: beat@allonetribedrum.com
Fax: 505-751-0509

Black Swamp Percussion
2341 Linden Drive
Adrian, MI 49221
voice + fax 517.263.1364
http://www.blackswamp.com/bswamp/
email: info@blackswamp.com

International Percussion Imports
Features percussion instruments from South America.
PO Box 464
Columbus, GA 31902
1-800-418-9793
http://members.aol.com/intlimport/index.html

Lark in the Morning
Well-established mail order company specializing in exotic instruments.
For the 100-page Lark Catalog send $3.00 in the US, $6.00 elsewhere to
Lark In The Morning PO Box 1176, Mendocino, CA 95460 USA
LarkInfo: (707) 964-3762
Mail Order (707) 964-5569
Fax (707) 964-1979
Mendocino Retail Showroom:(707) 937-LARK
Seattle Retail Showroom:(206) 623-3440
http://www.mhs.mendocino.k12.ca.us/MenComNet/Business/Retail/Larkne
t/larkhp.html
email larkinam@larkinam.com

Pro Drum
A fairly extensive line of drums and percussion instruments
from Africa, Middle East, Asia, and South America
363 North Easton Rd.
Glenside, PA 19038
215-887-1462
215-887-3793
http://www.prodrum.com/contents.htm
email: info@prodrum.com

Rhythm Makers
Handcrafted, tunable hand drums by Master Drummaker Doug Powell.
Ashikos, frame drums, and djuns djuns (or doundoun) with many exceptional qualities.
1-800-308-7841
http://www.pimps.com/retail/drums.html
email address: yaelhana@ipa.net

Iñaki Sebastián Mallets
Camino Okendotegi, 40 bajo (Casa Aránzazu)
20115 ASTIGARRAGA (Guipúzcoa) SPAIN
Tel. (0034-43) 33 12 41
*****
Marcelo Celayeta, 72 – 3°A
31014 PAMPLONA (Navarra) SPAIN
Fax (0034-48) 14 27 18
Web site includes pages in English, Spanish and French.
http://www.cin.es/mallets/
email: mallets@cin.es

ThunderHeart Drums
John Millen, Master Drummaker
Handmade ashikos, frame drums, council drums; makes drums to order, too.
4437 Clifton Road
Baltimore, Maryland USA
21216
http://www.abs.net/~jmillen/
email: thunderheart@pobox.com

Bibliography

Berendt, Joachim Ernst. *Ich höre, also ich bin.* Munich: Goldmann Verlag.

—. *The Third Ear.* New York: Henry Holt & Co., 1992.

Canacakis-Canacs, J. "Pyrovasy – The Non-Burning Phenomenon," *Music and Medicine 8.*, 1976.

Cousto, Hans. *The Cosmic Octave.* Mendocino: LifeRhythm, 1988.

Diamond, John. *Lebensenergie in der Musik, Band 1.* Südergellersen: Verlag Bruno Martin, 1994.

Flatischler, Reinhard. *Der Weg zum Rhythmus.* Synthesis.

—. *The Forgotten Power of Rhythm.* Mendocino: LifeRhythm, 1992.

Giger, Peter. *Die Kunst des Rhythmus.* Mainz: Schott Musik International.

Hamel, Peter Michael. *Through Music to the Self: How to Appreciate and Experience Music Anew.* Boulder: Shambala, 1979.

Hart, Mickey with Jay Stevens. *Drumming at the Edge of Magic: A Journey into the Spirit of Percussion.* SanFrancisco: HarperSanFrancisco, 1990.

Hegi, Fritz. *Improvisation und Musiktherapie.* Paderborn: Junfermann Verlag.

Heimrath, Johannes. *Das Sonogram der Persönlichkeit: Gongs als Modulatoren der Körperenergie.* Munich: Heinrich Hugendubel Verlag.

Jahn, Janheinz. *Muntu: African Culture and the Western World.* New York: Grove Weidenfeld, 1961.

Jansen, Eva Rudy. *Singing Bowls.* Diever, Holland: Binkey Kok Publications, 1990.

Kapteina, Hartmut. *Musical Group Improvisation: Musicotherapeutic Work in Social Services.* Essays, 1976-1991.

Leonard, George. *Der Rhythmus des Kosmos.* Reinbek bei Hamburg: Rowohlt Verlag.

Meyberg, Wolfgang. *Trommelnderweise: Trommeln in Therapie und Selbsterfahrung.* Grosser Bär, 1989.

Moreno, Joseph. "The Music Therapist as Shaman" *Musicotherapeutic Review*, Vol. 8, No. 2., 1987.

Priestly, M. *Experience in Music Therapy.* Stuttgart: Gustav Fischer Verlag, 1982.

Schellberg, Dirk. *Didgeridoo.* Diever, Holland: Binkey Kok Publications, 1994.

Timmerman, Tonius: *Music as a Path.* Herten: Pan Tao Musikverlag, 1987.

Tomatis, Alfred A. *Der Klang des Lebens*. Reinbek bei Hamburg: Rowohlt Verlag.
—. *The Conscious Ear: My Life of Transformation Through Listening*. Barrytown, NY: Station Hill, 1992.

Index